Dope Fiction
Alpha Female
Antwan Floyd Sr.

Dedicated 2

Hustlers that move beyond maintaining to the level of exceeding

Antwan Floyd Sr.

BLACK LOVE DETECTIVE NOVELS
Piece Keeper
Cannibal in the City
Body Bags & Last Rites
A Pound of Flesh, An Ounce of Blood
The Detective and the Criminal
The 13th Prospect Stranded on Stony Island

Paperbacks:
Crew Love
Crew Love pt. 2 "The Black Mob"
Dope Fiction "Alpha Female"
Dope Fiction pt. 2 "Sigma Female"
Dope Fiction pt. 3 Beta Female
Wild 100's
Sperm Donor
Danielle Lovelace Vigilante for Hire
Purple Reign "A Trigger Brown Mystery"
Dead Before Morning "Rhys & Tilly Series Book 1"
The Addiction "An Anthology"

Ebooks:
The Last Transmission of a Gangster
12 Months of Murder: Introduction to Seduction
12 Months of Murder: Reasonable Doubt
12 Months of Murder: The Life and Times of Jade Leskiv Vol. 1

Prologue
Early 90's

Whip sat behind the wheel of her 91 Cutlass; Danesha sat next to her in the passenger seat rolling a blunt. Nicole and Carlene both sat in the back seat.

"How long do we have to wait on her to get here?" Carlene asked referring to Cheyenne. She was the final member of their five girl crew.

"You know we can't leave without here." Whip snapped, turning down the volume on the radio.

"Shit, why not she can stay here, and we can take Nick." Carlene spat back.

"Nah, Nick ain't cut out for that."

Carlene laughed. "And she's ready to start copping alone right?"

"I made the decision Carlene were not discussing it." Whip was the leader. Not necessarily because she was the toughest but more because she had elements of all of them within her psyche. She was a real hustler like Danesha, loyal like Nicole, a killer like Cheyenne, and a gangster like Carlene. Carlene often bumped heads with Whip, nothing personal just always testing her to see if she would bend or break.

"You'll do fine Nick." Whip said looking at her in the backseat through the rearview mirror. Nicole remained silent, nodding at Whip with an assured stature about herself.

"Yeah, as long as she can stay off the bottle." Danesha added as she lit the blunt and took a pull. Nicole rolled her eyes.

"You can stay here and I can go to Illinois if you think you can do better." Nicole snapped back. She was the youngest of the group only 19 years old. She found herself always having to fight for respect of the group. It was true she had a drinking problem she would never admit that to her girls especially not to Danesha or Carlene.

"You ain't never killed nothing." Danesha said handing the blunt to Whip.

"What that mean I'm supposed to be scared? The shit ain't hard."

"We done talking about this shit Danesha and Carlene leave the girl alone damn; you bitches is worrisome as hell sometimes. Nick get the shit put it up, wait till we get back."

"Alright." She responded folding her arms across her chest.

"Cool, now get your ass out my car Cheyenne just pulled up."

Nicole did as she was told climbing out as Cheyenne climbed in and sat in her place. Nicole stood watching as the car crept away leaving her standing alone.

***

The wind whistled and howled as Nicole pulled at the straps of her quarter length butter soft leather coat. A matching leather bag over her shoulder. She stuck her hands in her pockets as she rushed into the neighborhood lounge. Pausing to give the security guard a kiss on the cheek she slipped three nicely folded one-hundred dollar bills into his hand. For the three bills he skipped the pat down, and she walked right in with her .38 snub. With a wink and a nod, she was off to her favorite booth in the corner of the bar. Nicole was a hustler in a crew of female hustlers. They earned a certain degree of respect that was equal if, not above the handful of top Black male hustlers in the city. They earned well and knew how to keep their mouth shut, so it wasn't unheard of for the local Costa Nostra to hire them to do certain favors from time to time. Everyone had a position to play, and Nicole played hers well. She could play all the parts that needed filling when they needed to be filled. She could fight and could sell it all from girl, coke, and weed to stolen cars, clothes, and information. She could turn coke to crack pretty well, though not as well as Whip, she got the job done regardless.

***

She was riding solo tonight because the other girls had to drive to Chicago for a job they were doing for Whip's brother. Even though she didn't go she would still get a split. She'd just come from copping three kilos. She knew she should have gone straight to the stash house but figured she would stop off for drinks first. Nicole sat at her favorite table drinking shot after shot and turning down offers to dance by her many admirers. She was very nice to look at only 19 years old and barely five feet her beautiful brown skin glowed no matter what the lighting in the room was like. Dark brown bedroom eyes she illuminated beauty where ever she went. She was accustomed to all eyes being on her just as they were tonight.

Ickie was no exception. He'd spotted her the moment she entered the room. He sent over a bottle of champagne to let her know he was scoping her. Ickie was an associate of her crew. He ran different scams here and there and had been trying to get with Nicole for a quite a while. He wasn't a bad looking man. Most of the women in the hood wanted him, but he just wasn't Nicole's type. Ickie was determined to change her viewpoint. He made his way to her table as the waitress popped the cork on the five hundred dollar bottle of liquor. Before she could pour a glass, he retrieved the bottle from the waitress and shooed her off.

"How long you been working here?" Nicole asked jokingly as she picked up the glass and held it for him to pour the champagne.

Ickie poured the drink and the champagne bubbled running over the glass and spilling onto Nicole's hand. Setting the bottle on the table, he quickly took her wet hand and slowly licked the champagne from her fingers.

Nicole pulled from his grasp as she wiped the excess alcohol from her hand with a cloth napkin. "Thank you, for the drink...and the foreplay," she said sarcastically.

"My pleasure, Nick. Where the rest of your girls at?"

Nicole placed a cigarette in her mouth, lit it, took a puff and blew the smoke in Ickie's direction. "Why?"

"Cause I asked."

Nicole turned her head away from Ickie. No longer paying him any attention she began nodding her head to the music. Ickie silently eased away from her table as he watched a man slide into the booth next to Nicole and pour himself a glass of the champagne he had just bought. He stared at the two. He felt himself getting angrier with each shot he watched her take. She played him and she would pay. She'll be too drunk to even know what hit her, he thought as he formed a plan in his head. The night progressed slowly from then on as he watched guy after guy get shot down by Nicole. The alcohol was starting to take its effect on her and the vultures were circling as they watched her stumble towards the door. Ickie slithered in her direction opening his suit jacket flashing the butt of his gun at a brother looking a little too overprotective beside her. Upon seeing the gun, the guy quickly backed down. Ickie then took Nicole by the arm.

She looked up ready to scold him then stopped once she realized who it was. "Oh, Ickie, thank you. These brothers in here like...like..."

"Dogs in heat."

Nicole laughed. "Yeah, they found the wrong bitch tonight though."

Ickie chuckled.

She continued to slur. "You are so sweet, Ickie."

Sweet? He thought. Fuck sweet. He guided her towards her car and blocking out whatever it was that she was rambling on about. He paid extra attention to her clutching tight to the leather bag. The gesture piqued his interest. "Where your keys at?" he asked as he reached for her bag.

She pulled back from his grasp. "Backup, Ickie." She quickly dug into her bag and pulled out the .38. "Bang, bang!" She mimicked the sound of a quick round before laughing. Seeing that Ickie was unfazed she waved the gun once more, still laughing, then dropped the weapon back in her purse before grabbing her car keys.

"Girl, you silly as hell." Ickie looked at her cautiously.

She fumbled with the key chain before managing to unlock the door, open it and climb in behind the wheel. She closed the door, put the key in the ignition, and turned the engine.

Ickie stood outside the car tapping on her car window. Nicole hit the down button and as the window rolled down, he peered inside. "You shouldn't be driving."

"I'm fine."

"At least let me call someone."

"Thanks but..."

"Let me ride home with you and I can catch a cab from..."

Nicole rolled her eyes and grunted in frustration. "Get in man, damn."

Ickie rushed around to the passenger's seat before she could change her mind, opened the door, and got in. Quickly Nicole pulled off into traffic before he could close the door.

***

Nicole woke up in a hotel room fully clothed lying in bed. Her head was spinning. Slowly she sat up in bed as she tried to figure out where she was and how she had gotten there. She was alone as far as she could tell. Bits and pieces of the night came back to her in a blur. She thought about Ickie. Had he gotten the room for her? Did he try to do anything to her? She looked down and checked her clothes. Other than her missing shoes nothing on her was out of place, not even a button undone. Her mouth felt dry and her stomach was growling. Sliding from the bed, she observed the room. She felt panic sweep over her as she moved about desperately looking for her leather bag. How could I have been so stupid? She thought as she burst into the bathroom. Stopping in her tracks, she stood with her mouth agape as her eyes fell upon Ickie laid out in the tub with her gun on top of him and the leather bag thrown carelessly on the tiled floor.

Ignoring the body in the tub she went straight for the leather bag. "No, no, no!" She murmured to herself repeatedly as she paced the small bathroom. She was unable to recall an enormous portion of the night and she had no idea how she had ended up there nor what she could do to fix her current predicament. A knock at the door took her out of her trance. Nicole rushed to the door shaking with anxiety. "Yeah?"

"Housekeeping."

"Not now. I'm staying an extra day."

The woman didn't say another word. Nicole put her ear to the door and listened as she heard the cart move away from the door and the housekeeper knock on another door. She returned to the bathroom being careful not to touch anything. She let her eyes scour the area looking for her missing merchandise from the leather bag. Making her way back to the room, she sat at the desk and thought about her next move. Only one name came to mind. Courtney Awsum. He had once told her that should she ever need anything she could count on him. She couldn't go to her girls. She'd lost three bricks of cocaine and had a dead man in the tub. On top of that she had no idea how either happened. She'd had one job: cop the coke and put it up. Whip was supposed cook it when they got back from Chicago. Maybe the girls were right when they'd previously warned her that she had a drinking problem. But it was too late to dwell on that now. All out of options, she picked up the phone and called Courtney.

Thirty minutes later Nicole found herself forcing down coffee as she waited impatiently. She really needed a drink. After calling Courtney, she had called down to the desk to book the room for another night which proved to be yet another mistake on her part once she found out that the room was in Ickie's name. She'd quickly hung up and called Courtney back to inform that there was one more problem for him to fix. Nicole was no fool she knew that no one did anything from the kindness of their heart but, whatever the price he asked, if he brought her out of this winning she would gladly pay whatever.

Her nerves were on edge as she stood in the bathroom entrance and stared at Ickie's lifeless frame. What the hell did he do to make me do this? She thought to herself. She whipped her head in the direction of the door as the sound of knocking took her out of her trance. Please let that be Courtney, she silently prayed to herself as she rushed to the door.

"Who is it?" She stood in front of the white painted steel door and yelled at the presence on the other side. Anxiety was killing her.

"It's me!" A deep baritone voice answered back.

She snatched the door open and walked away not looking back to see if he was alone which he wasn't. He was followed by a man and a woman both wheeling in suitcases behind them.

"Nick, these are my associates," Courtney explained bringing her attention to the tag-alongs. "Do as they say and everything should flow smoothly."

Nicole nodded yes as she began biting her nails.

"Good." The woman with a British accent was relieved that there would be no resistance. She picked up her suitcase, sat it on the bed, and removed new clothes and shoes. The tags were still on the garments. She handed the clothes to Nicole. "Go change. Do a quick wash in the sink of all visible areas. Hands up to your elbows, face, neck, behind your ears. Any place that may have blood splatter."

Nicole was astonished. "Blood splatter? I didn't kill this guy!"

Courtney raised his eyebrow at her defensive outburst. "Are you going to do what they say or are you going to debate your innocence?" He was obviously annoyed.

Nicole made her way to the bathroom and closed the door behind her. Ten minutes later she was changed holding her old clothes in her hand. The man who had yet to speak opened a black hefty garbage bag and Nicole promptly dropped the clothes into it.

Courtney took her by the arm and led her to the door. "Go out into the hall, bypass the elevator straight to the end of the hallway and get onto the service elevator. Take it down to the basement. Get off of the elevator and take a left. Walk until you see a black caravan. The door will be unlocked. Get into the van. The keys are in the ignition. Drive yourself home." His instructions were precise. Courtney was thorough if nothing else and could not omit the last bit of information Nicole needed. "I couldn't get the product you are missing in such short notice but underneath the passenger seat of the van is a bag of cash. It's the money you spent on the product."

Nicole let out a sigh of relief. "Thank you so much, Courtney. I owe you one. I'll pay you back every penny."

Courtney nodded. "I know you will. The money part I know you're good for it and as far as the mess in the bathroom... I know if I ever need anything you got me."

"Anything! Just ask." She gave him a hug and sighed once more as he kissed her forehead. It was all so perfect. "Courtney?"

"Yes?"

"Can we keep this between us? Whip and the other girls don't need to know."

He smiled. "Not a problem."

***

Whip dropped her travel bag on the floor near the door. She'd just made it back into Indy from the business trip to Chicago. Exhausted she shed her clothes dropping them on the floor as she made her way to the bathroom to take a shower. She turned on the bathroom light then turned the water on in the shower. Letting the water run Whip stood nude in the center of the toilet looking at her reflection in the mirror hanging on the wall. Her mocha complexion was complemented nicely by her soft curly hair. She climbed into the shower just as the bathroom began to fill with steam. After a few minutes of basking in the warmth of the steady flowing stream, she heard banging on her front door. Hopping out of the tub she wrapped herself in a towel she rushed to the door.

"Who is it?" She hollered as she tore down the hallway. She was annoyed that someone would have the audacity to interrupt her moment of tranquility.

"Courtney."

Whip paused in mid-step upon hearing the response. She bit her bottom lip and considered the reason for his abrupt visit. Getting over her apprehension she took the final four steps to the door and opened it. "Sorry. I was in the shower." She turned away and headed back to her bedroom.

Courtney entered the apartment then closed and locked the door. "It's alright. Didn't mean to be an imposition but I stopped by 'cause I needed to talk to you about something important."

"I'm listening," she yelled from her bedroom with the door wide open.

Courtney stood at the head of the hallway and hollered back towards Whip's open door. "It's about Nick." No longer concerned with decorum Courtney made his way down the hall towards her bedroom. He stood in the doorway and took in the scene. She had one foot on the bed and one on the floor as she applied lotion to her leg.

Whip made a few exaggerated movements as she glided her hand up and down her calf being sure to part her legs to give him a full view of her freshly shaven vagina. She paused and looked up at him with bare flesh glistening from the lotion. "Uh, excuse me. Can I help you?" She had a hint of attitude in her tone.

Courtney took his time examining her body. Starting at her feet his eyes scoured every inch of her mocha frame. "Yeah, you can help me." He walked into the room like a black panther about to mate with his female counterpart. He picked her up by her waist and threw her onto the bed.

She stared back venomously. Her nostrils flared and she felt goose bumps race across her flesh in response to his touch. Like a wild animal, she pounced from the bed landing on his chest. She wrapped her legs around his midsection and one arm around his neck to hold herself up. She dug her nails into his neck with her free hand until blood ran freely. Courtney pulled her by her hair yanking her neck back then suckled its taunt skin so fiercely she thought he might suck a vein out. They both grunted in ecstasy as he fell forward on top of her onto the bed.

After the third romp of their impromptu sexual escapade, they both lay nude with the blanket halfway on the bed and halfway on the floor. Staring at the ceiling they took turns puffing a joint lost in their own thoughts. The sex was just as good as Whip thought it would be a problem in and of itself was because it meant she would want more. If he was feeling her as much as she was feeling him then, there was an even bigger problem because that meant there would be more escapades. In her line of business, she couldn't afford to get caught up in emotions and desires. Not wanting to think about it further nor ruin the serene mood she broke the silence. "What did you need to tell me about Nicole?"

Courtney scooped her into his arms and held her to his chest. "Never mind."

Whip pushed against his chest prying herself from his grasp. She sat up. "Whatever. You wanted something. You didn't just pop up over her to seduce me."

He rolled over, turning his back to her. "Don't act like you didn't want this to happen."

She pushed the back of his head smashing his face into the pillow. "Just 'cause I wanted it, ain't mean it had to go down."

Courtney sat up and rose from the bed. "So it shouldn't have gone down?"

She stared up at him and watched his pole begin to extend. She gasped as it started to pulsate. She was silently in awe.

"Are we going talk about this or are you going to stare at my dick?" He was taunting her.

Upset she climbed from the bed and stood directly in front of him. Staring up into his eyes she angrily poked his bare chest. "Talk about this? Who you fooling? You didn't come over here to talk to me." Without another word, she slyly knelt down taking his jones directly into her mouth and sucked as if he were lactating.

Present Day

Kill the brain, the body must die!

~Cheyenne

"Thank you again, Governor Love. This is an excellent book!" The female patron gushed as Ally Love signed a copy of her latest title "Dust off the Ashes."

"My pleasure. And please call me Ally. I'm not your Governor anymore." She handed the book to the woman and smiled.

"No disrespect, Ally, but you have done more for the people in this city in the years you were in office than anyone has done in the past twenty years. And your new book..." The woman held the book close to her chest. "Dust off the Ashes will be a best seller and the fact that you're donating all the proceeds to the battered women's shelter proves that you are a God send. For that and everything else you've done you will always be my Governor."

Ally hugged the woman. "Thank you. I sincerely hope you enjoy the book."

The woman turned and exited the Oakley Auditorium in Ivy Tech's Community College clutching the novel as if it were a sacred heirloom. The college had hosted for a lecture and book signing. Both had gone well, but now things were wrapping up. She looked around the auditorium for her husband. Late again, she thought to herself. Checking her IPHONE for any missed messages she saw that there were none. Dropping the phone into her purse, she began packing her laptop into her bag to leave.

"What's good, Whip?" A voice called from the seats.

Ally's back was to the seating area and she could feel the hairs on the back of her neck stand up. She hadn't gone by the street moniker in over twenty years. Who would dare address her as such in this arena? She turned around smiling half-heartedly as she placed her hand in front of her face in an attempt to block the spotlight that was

14

shining in her eyes. She remained silent as she watched the shadowy figure carrying a knapsack approach the stage. When the person was near enough for Ally to get a clear view, she tore away from the stage abandoning her belongings. The first thing she noticed was that she was wearing black from head to toe. Black hoodie, jeans, boots and leather gloves. She also wore the four karat canary yellow diamond earrings she had given her one year for her birthday. Ally was shocked. "Oh my God! When did you get home?" She threw her arms around the woman in a strong embrace.

"A couple hours ago."

"Thank God, he brought you back home to us."

"I'm home alright. It had nothing to do with God though."

Ally took a step back and looked at her old friend. She smiled. "In any case it's good to see you, I see you still have the earrings."

Cheyenne ran both hands across the diamonds in her earlobes. "How are the rest of the girls?"

"Oh God... we haven't gotten together since... well you know... since you went away."

"I went away huh?" Cheyenne's eyebrow rose. "Like a breeze in the wind."

Ally tried to keep her tone even. "I wrote you and put money on your books. Why did you take my name off of the visiting list?"

"I was doing my time. I didn't need anyone to do that time with me. I jumped in front of that bullet, Whip."

"Don't be so bleak, Cheyenne." Ally looked around at the few stragglers that were still in the auditorium. "And I don't go by Whip anymore. Just call me Ally. Those days are behind me."

Cheyenne took a step back and looked at Ally analyzing her eyes and face. "Ally. Right. It's a real shame though, Whip." She held her hands up as if she were mixing ingredients in a pot over the stove. "When you was in that kitchen, you had the best whip game out there. Hit the product with a little water, baking soda, and bam! Man, you turned a thousand grams into a brick and a half every rip and it still tasted like butter."

Ally felt her skin crawl listening to Cheyenne reminisce about the old days.

Cheyenne paused noticing her old buddy's discomfort. She smiled with dark eyes. "But yeah, those days are behind you. Me, I don't know so much."

Ally turned to retrieve her things. "Well, you came here for a reason, Cheyenne. So what's up?"

Cheyenne chuckled. "Still the same ol' Whip. Straight to the point right?"

Ally's eyes narrowed and her nose flared at the blatant disrespect. "Some shit don't change huh?" she asked in a hushed tone between clenched teeth. "Same ol' Cheyenne shitting on whoever doing whatever she wants."

"Yeah well, I suppose some people don't change. You know we all can't trade in two-hundred dollar jeans for two thousand dollar suits. When it comes to people like me, no matter what, once a gangster always a gangster. 'Ya feel me?"

Ally didn't like where the conversation was headed and attempted to pass Cheyenne to exit the stage area. "If you say so. It was nice seeing you, but I have to go."

Cheyenne blocked her path.

Ally took a step back and stared at the other woman aggressively. She had always been the less skilled fighter of the crew but was undoubtedly the one with the most heart and was always the first one to run to a fight. "Move, Cheyenne."

"Not before I'm done."

Ally placed her hands on her hips. "Well, speak your peace so I can be on my way."

Cheyenne held up both of her hands in a non-defensive manner. "I just want an autograph."

Ally stared back disbelievingly.

Cheyenne chuckled. "Straight up, Whip."

Ally shot her a nasty look. The doors resounded throughout the empty room as the last attendees exited. Ally felt uncomfortable.

"I mean, Ally, just an autograph." Cheyenne spoke with mock sincerity. "Seriously."

Letting down her guard, she attempted to pass Cheyenne once more and pointed to a box sitting on a tote bag sitting in a chair in the front row of the stadium seats. "Let me get you a book."

Cheyenne blocked her again.

Ally was annoyed. "Ugh, what is this, Cheyenne? I don't have time to-"

Cheyenne reached into the army fatigue knapsack she was carrying and removed a copy of Ally's book. "I brought my own."

Ally felt a little guilty about her behavior. It had been almost two decades since they'd last seen one another. She had forgotten how aggressive Cheyenne's personality was. Placing her hand on her forehead Ally laughed nervously. "Girl, I'm sorry. I'm tripping." Ally quickly pulled out a pen and signed the book before handing it back to Cheyenne. "I didn't think you would read stuff like this."

"Usually don't. Just stuff about human nature and the natural laws of nature shit." Cheyenne looked down at the novel and stepped to the side.

Ally passed her laughing. "Shit like that huh?"

"Yeah. Shit. Like...you know."

Amused Ally paused and turned back to face Cheyenne. "Enlighten me on shit, as you so elegantly put it."

Cheyenne swung the hardcover book smacking Ally square across the temple with the flat side of the book. Ally's head involuntarily jerked to the side as a second blow with the spine of the book smashed against her windpipe. Falling backward clutching at her throat Cheyenne throttled her pummeling her throat with ferocious blows until her windpipe cracked. "Enlighten you? Huh, smart mouth bitch? Everyone knows you kill the brain, the body must die!"

My word, not yours.

~Danesha Andrews

Carmen Wheeler stepped off of her school bus clutching her book bag. The 13-year-old girl chatted with friends as she made her way to the front door of the duplex she lived in with her mother. Carmen was a latchkey child. Her mother worked two jobs so she spent most days and nights home alone. Carmen waved goodbye to her girlfriends and as they kept walking she slid the key into the lock. She unlocked the door, pushed it open, and stepped in. Carmen was oblivious to the detective watching her in an unmarked car parked across the street from her house.

He picked up his radio and spoke through it as the young girl closed the oak door behind her. "Yeah, the girl just went in."

"Look like anyone following her? "A female voice asked back through the radio.

"She's alone. Just like yesterday, the day before yesterday, and every day last week."

"You don't have to be here." The female associate shot back at him. She wasn't in the mood for attitude.

"It's not a problem."

"Then what's the bitching for?"

"We have been coming here and waiting and looking for hours for this jerk off. I don't think he's going to show."

She sighed deeply through the radio. "Trust me, Aiello."

"I trust you with my life. Shit, you're my partner. But if the Captain finds out she's going to shit bricks." Aiello sat for a few seconds. After no response, he spoke on the radio once more. "Danesha?" Still no answer. He dropped the radio, opened his car door, jumped out and ran across the street to Carmen's door. Pulling his gun from the holster, he banged on the door. "Police! Open the door!"

He hesitated for a moment before kicking the door in. Moving quickly into the apartment, he moved towards the voices. He heard shrills from a girl and a man grunting. Now in the back of the house in the dining room he saw Carmen in the corner crying and his partner with her knee in Morgan Fowlkes back with her gun to his head.

"Get her out of here!" Danesha yelled as she placed the handcuffs on Morgan.

Aiello did as he was told. He walked around his partner and the perp to reach the girl. Placing his arm around her trembling body, he guided her towards the door. Once they were gone Danesha pulled Morgan to his feet and put her gun back into its holster.

"It will never stick bitch!" Morgan yelled with a sly grin plastered across his face.

Danesha ignored his rants of insults as she unbuckled his belt, unbuttoned then unzipped his pants, and pulled them down to his ankles.

"Yeah, that's what I'm talking about," Morgan cooed in sick perverted manner. "You're a little too old for me but daddy will do you right too. Take these cuffs off me and let me get it right."

Danesha stepped back and watched him begin to rise. She felt her stomach churn with disgust. "Get it right, huh?" She placed her hands on her hips.

"Damn right! Get these things off me."

Danesha stepped closer. The man was now thoroughly aroused. Taking her left hand she grasped his Johnson digging her nails into his flesh.

He squealed as his hips jerked forward being led by the detective. "Damn, girl! Not so rough with the merchandise."

She pulled out her Taser with her right hand and jabbed the probes directly onto his balls pressing the button with no mercy. The electrical current shot through his body. As he tried to get away, she clutched tighter at his penis keeping the Taser pressed against his genitals. He screamed out in pain until he could no longer take it. Finally, he dropped to his knees and passed out.

***

Danesha stepped into her precinct followed by her partner, Aiello. They were greeted with cheers, applause, and pats on the back as they made their way through the crowd to their desks. Sitting in her chair Danesha took her gun off and dropped it in her bottom drawer. Rocking back in the chair, she began to look through folders of open cases that she had been working on.

"Andrews! Un-ass that seat. You too, Aiello! Both of you in my office!" The Lieutenant was fuming as she yelled at them from down the hall. She gave a menacing stare then turned and walked back into her office.

Aiello, whose desk was right across from Danesha's, leaned over and whispered. "I told you."

Danesha rolled her eyes and smiled. "It was worth it." She stood to her feet and followed her partner into they're lieutenant's office.

"Close the door, Detective." Lieutenant Monet she stood behind her desk still fuming. The short curly redhead with a thick Irish accent removed her glasses placing the tip of the temple arms in her mouth. She chewed it for a few seconds before speaking. "Hmmm. What should I do with you two?"

"I don't know about her, but I could use a raise," Aiello said attempting to lighten the mood.

"A raise? Really? You are about this close to unemployment, Aiello." Lieutenant Monet held her thumb and pointer finger close together.

"He was just backing my play, boss." Danesha wasn't about to let her partner take the heat for her decisions.

"Your play?"

"Yes, Ma'am."

"Your play as you put it landed a man in the ICU."

Danesha smirked.

Lieutenant Monet was not amused. "This is funny? Wipe that stupid smile off your face."

The smile slowly faded morphing into a cynical scowl.

"Do you know how tall I am, detective?" Lieutenant Monet pointed her glasses at Danesha.

"Excuse me, ma'am?" Danesha was confused.

"My height! You're a detective. A first-year beat cop can give a physical description for heaven's sake."

"5'4, ma'am."

"5'4. That's right."

"I don't follow," Aiello said trying to understand where the questioning was going.

"5'4, detectives. 145, maybe 155, pounds. I can assure you that it does not feel good to have a Captain crawling up your ass!"

"Liu—"

"Shut your mouth! I have been on the phone with Internal affairs, human rights advocacy attorneys...Dodging calls from damn reporters looking for a story of police harassment and brutality. Tell me why I shouldn't have both of your badges in my desk drawer as we speak?"

"He got what he deserved." Danesha shrugged and surveyed the dirt underneath her fingernails.

"I have to agree with her, lieutenant. That scum bag baby rapist got everything he deserved. We should've dropped him in a hole."

"That will be enough, detective."

Danesha was pleased by her partner's defense. "I'm with Aiello on this one."

"And I said enough!" Monet banged her knuckles down on the desk cracking the lenses of the reading glasses she'd been clutching. "Aiello, out! We'll talk later. Andrews sit!"

Aiello promptly exited the office slamming the door closed behind him. Danesha sat.

"You are a good detective," Lieutenant Monet stated.

"Thank you, Lieutenant."

Monet walked around to the front of her desk and stood over Danesha. "No, I take that back. You are a damn good detective." She shook her head in solace. "But this stunt is going to piss it all away. What were you thinking, Andrews?"

"I was thinking I wasn't going to let him get away with this."

"Instincts! Instincts, every good cop has them, relies on them, and uses them especially out in the field. So you're telling me, Andrews, that somewhere waaaaaay in the back of your mind you didn't hear a little voice saying 'stop, don't do it... this is more trouble than it's worth?"

"Do what?"

"Don't screw with me, Andrews."

"I have no idea what you're talking about?"

"You didn't put the shock to his ding dong?"

"No, ma'am."

"This is narcotics," Monet stating spreading her arms wide. "What in the hell were you even doing at this residence in the first place? We don't scope out sex offenders over here. We scope out drug lords and cartels."

"We were following up on a lead." Danesha had her story ready.

"A lead?"

"Yes, ma'am. A snitch of mine put us up on a meth lab on the East Side."

Lieutenant Monet sucked her teeth. "Bullshit! You better come up with a better story than that for I-A."

"I'm not worried about the rat squad." Danesha's demeanor remained hard.

"The media's gonna have a field day with this one."

"I'm willing to deal with that too."

"I'm not."

Danesha began to speak, but the Lieutenant cut her off. "Like I said, you're a hell of a cop. I knew that when you transferred from homicide a year ago. I don't give a damn about the rumors and the rumblings. If you're dirty, you're dirty and I'll find out soon enough I always do. As long as you bring down the big cases and don't play me like an ass you'll always have a place in narcotics. I do whatever I can to look out for my people." There was a brief moment of silence before Monet stood to her feet and rounded the desk back to her seat. "All I ask is that you shoot straight with me."

Danesha took that as her cue to leave. She rose from her seat and cleared her throat. "Last year right before I transferred to narcotics I was working a body I caught on the west side. My lieutenant paired me up with a detective working a sexual abuse case. Our cases were connected. We were trying to flip Morgan Fowlkes. He raped the daughter of his girlfriend at the time. It was his cousin we suspected of the murder in my case. Long story short we never did flip him and my case went cold. The rape case on Fowlkes went to trial, he got a slap on the wrist and was hit with a year in county. The look on that little girl's face when she took the stand and testified...I still see her face when I go to bed at night. I promised her I would never let him near her again."

Lieutenant Monet felt her heart shift. "You've been a cop for how long now, Andrews? You know we can't make promises like that to victims."

"How I came up your word was all you had. It was mine. Not the departments and not Aiello's. My word, not yours. And badge or no badge I was going to keep it. And I did."

.....and mama loved papa.

~Nicolai

Nicolai sat behind the wheel of the Mercedes-Benz CLA 250. He inhaled the scent of fresh leather and wood. His thoughts wandered as he thought about the trip he had to take to pick up his cousin. He dreaded the three-hour ride to Michigan. His cousin was being released from prison today and he'd gotten him a job at a warehouse. With the window slightly cracked he turned the stereo to 93.1 WIBC news talk radio. Half listening to the commentator talk about the recent case of some football player in legal troubles he tuned into the conversation taking place outside of the car. Kendricks, a guy he had met in Ohio while in county jail, was handling some business. Kendricks had hooked him up with a management job. Previously Nicolai had sold weight to the different neighborhood hustlers on the East and West sides of Indy. He'd made decent money but nothing like Kendricks made.

Nicolai looked at his reflection in the rearview mirror. Shaking his head in disgust, he felt like a failure. I am almost twice his age and here I am driving him around in his car while he runs his errands, he thought. To top it all off he's Black! Things have to turn around. Nicolai continued to listen to Kendricks talking on his cell phone. He turned the volume up on the radio as he watched a boy approach. He couldn't have been any older than twelve years old and was carrying a puppy. Kendricks handed the boy some cash and took the animal. He shook the boy's hand and got into the car. Setting the puppy on his lap he closed the door and Nicolai pulled off.

"Nice coat. What breed is he?" Nicolai asked as he turned the corner leaving the block.

"American Pit Bull Terrier. Full blooded. Thinking about breeding 'em."

"How you know he's full blooded?"

"I trust the kid."

"Kids lie too. How much you pay for him?"

"Why?" Kendricks was becoming annoyed.

"Just asking."

"No one just asks anything."

Nicolai grunted.

"Don't you trust anyone?" Kendricks questioned

"I try not to."

"Lonely world you live in, Nicolai."

He shrugged. "When I was about two or three years younger than that boy I lived in New York. Me, my mama, and papa."

Kendricks silently listened as he rubbed the puppy's belly.

Nicolai's eyes never left the road. "I have never seen a woman love a man more than Mama loved Papa. Not even from my own wife."

"Uh-huh."

"Papa was a ladies' man but Mama was no fool. She knew what Papa did in the streets. He took care of home though. Mama and I wanted for nothing and no woman ever approached Mama or disrespected our family in the street."

"What was the problem then?"

"Mama trusted Papa to do what Papa was going to do and not cross the line. Trust. It was all about trust. One day Mama caught Papa and the next door neighbor in bed sleep together. Of course, there was arguing and name calling between Mama and the woman. Papa diffused the situation and it never happened again...at least Papa never did it in their bed again. Three maybe four years passed and Papa was still the bread winner. We moved to a nicer neighborhood in Jersey. Beautiful big house. Mama and Papa both had excellent vehicles. Life was great. The very first night in the new house Mama made Papa's favorite meal, drew him a hot bath, and well... you know what a woman does for a husband to show her appreciation."

Kendricks laughed. "Yeah, I know. I have a wife of my own."

"Anyway, early the next morning while Papa was still asleep Mama quietly brought me into her room. She made me watch as she cut Papa's throat."

"Damn!" Kendricks hadn't expected such a harsh turn of events.

Nicolai didn't blink. "She didn't kill him. We both watched as he gurgled on his blood. She stopped the bleeding then sewed him right up. You asked me about trust. Mama trusted Papa and he hurt her. Papa trusted Mama and she hurt him. I ask you, trust who for what? People are hurt by those they trust. Mama cut Papa's throat and Mama loved Papa."

Kendricks remained silent as they pulled into the parking lot of the storage facility in Broad Ripple. A U-Haul truck pulled up behind them. Kendricks placed the puppy on the back seat and got out. The driver of the U-Haul got out and shook hands with Kendricks. The big Black man walked around to the rear of the truck followed by the driver. Kendricks slid the door open as the driver jumped up inside. The truck was filled with wooden crates covered by a logo of a black widow spider stamped. The man jumped down from the truck just as Nicolai turned the corner. Taken by surprise, the driver of the U-Haul reached for his gun. Nicolai paused as Kendricks grabbed his arm.

"Be cool, he's with me," Kendricks advised. "This is my mans. I told you about Nicolai."

"I don't give a damn who he is." The U-Haul driver was adamant. "Back the fuck up Nicole."

Nicolai looked passed him and into the truck.

"Fuck you looking at? I said beat it!" The driver held his gun at waist level.

"No problems, I'll wait over here." Nicolai stepped back and stood by the car. He could see the men but could not hear what they were saying.

Kendricks and the U-Haul driver stepped away another couple of feet and talked.

"Another fifty pounds for you Kendricks," the driver stated.

"Jesus Christ what is he storing all this crap for?"

"Just greed, man. He figures a drought will be hitting soon and when it does he'll take advantage of it and triple up on every kilo."

Kendricks shook his head smiling. "If he says so. Leave the keys to the U-Haul. I'll unload it and drop the truck off. Nicolai will take you back to your car."

"Does the boss know about this Nicolai guy?"

"Why would he? He's one of my guys. Been with us about a month or two now. He's been earning alright. Never late, never short."

"Hmm."

The men shook hands and the driver gave the keys to Kendricks. Together they walked back to the car where Nicolai patiently awaited them. The driver climbed into the passenger seat of the Benz.

"Do what he says, Nicolai," Kendricks ordered.

Nicolai nodded, got back to the car, and pulled off.

Rather revenged or avenged, when one feels wronged it's all done in passion.

~Danesha Andrews

"Hold his legs!" Danesha yelled as Aiello held Nicolai, a mid-level heroin dealer from the West Side, by his legs over the edge of a roof. "He can only hold you for so long, Nicolai. You really want to lose your life over a few dollars?"

"He slipping!" Aiello said as he began to lose his grip on the squirming and yelling Nicolai.

"Drop 'em." Danesha turned and began to walk away."

"See you on the other side." Aiello loosened his grip.

"No, no wait!" Nicolai yelled as his arms flailed in mid-air. "I'll tell you, I'll tell you! Pull me up."

Danesha took her time walking back to the edge of the roof. "Don't play with me, Nicolai. I don't have the time."

"I will! I'll tell you."

Danesha tapped her partner on the back giving him the okay to pull the man up. He dropped him on the roof top. Both men were sweating and panting.

"What's that smell?" Danesha scrunched up her nose as she grabbed her phone from her hip. A text message was coming through. "This little prick messed his pants."

"Screw you." Nicolai was embarrassed but grateful to still be alive. He wiped the sweat from his eyes with his sleeve.

Danesha paused to read her text message. Placing the phone back on her hip, she focused on Nicolai. "Where is it, Nicolai?"

He stared at her as if weighing his options.

She shot him a cold stare indicating that he had better uphold his end of the deal.

"A storage unit in Broad Ripple," he answered weakly.

"Don't make me have to come to you again. Next time it's not going to be as easy as dangling your ass over the side of a roof. I'm going to drive over to your nice fancy house out in Ohio that you think no one knows about. Gut that whale you call a wife and your dumb mute kid then draw a nice smiley face from ear to ear across her throat."

Nicolai dropped his head to his chest trying to shake off the horrific thoughts.

"We gave you a get out of jail free card when we busted you with those four ounces of smack in your trunk lest you forgot. We kept up our part of the deal. You keep up yours."

Nicolai nodded. "I will. I'll tell you."

"Make it good, Nicolai."

He sighed regretfully. "I have been riding around with this Kendricks guy lately. Never seen him touch anything but he is the real deal."

Aiello lit a cigarette. "Bullshit. I never heard of him."

"I swear to God I don't know how close he is to the man, but he is a lot closer than I will ever get."

"Tell me more about him. What does he look like? Kendricks, first name or last name?"

"Last name I think. Never got a first name. A Black guy. We were locked up together in Ohio. He was doing time for some misdemeanor... petty stuff... Think he caught a disorderly at a football game and beat up a few folks. One of 'em was an off duty cop. Spent a few days in jail before his lawyer got it all squashed."

"Why is he all buddy-buddy with you?"

"I knew a guy who knew a guy who did this thing for him. It worked out and he showed appreciation."

Danesha laughed. "You are so full of shit. What guy? What thing?"

"Doesn't matter."

"We're going to need more than that."

"I hear he does side deals." Nicolai was racking his brains for anything to get the vultures off of him. "He's been doing some recruiting out of Chicago and Gary."

"Your boy planning a little coup? Maybe he wants it all for himself."

"I don't know. I just hear things." He blinked fearfully. "Can I go?"

Aiello stomped out his cigarette and Danesha nodded. Nicolai stood to his feet and straightened out his clothes the best he could.

Danesha poked Nicolai in his chest. "I have business. Fill Aiello in more on this Kendricks guy and the storage unit."

Nicolai looked hurt but before either could respond Danesha was off and down the stairs to the street. Everyone hated Danesha. The guys she busted, the drug dealers she extorted, even her law enforcement co-workers who she undercut or outright double crossed to get career changing collars. She didn't care. She actually enjoyed it. The way she felt no matter what side of the law you were on it was all a stinking, rotting battlefield and when in war only the strong survived. Sometimes the lucky came out on top but that was rare and she wasn't going to leave her life in the hands of luck. Climbing into her pearl white Bugatti, she popped a freshly rolled grape flavored Swisher stuffed with platinum bubba Kush in her mouth. Swisher dangling between her lips she slid Kendrick Lamar's cd into the radio. As the music came on she turned the key and the car roared to life. She mashed the gas and took off towards Ivy Tech's community college. Twenty minutes and half a swisher later she was pulling into the parking lot. Walking past the yellow tape and bevy of uniformed officers, she made her way to the Oakley Auditorium. She flashed her badge to a uniformed officer guarding the door.

"What are you doing here Andrews?" A homicide detective questioned her suspiciously as she passed by. They were familiar with one another because she had worked the homicide unit for a year before transferring to narcotics.

"Beats me." She shrugged. "Jackson called me in." Spotting Detective Jackson across the room standing in front of the body as the medical examiner took photos of the crime scene. She made her way towards him.

Jackson suddenly looked up and spotting her he moved forward to meet her halfway. "Outside." He pointed for her to turn back around.

She opened her mouth to protest, but he grabbed her by the arm and led the way. Once outside, she pulled from his hold. "What's the deal?"

"Needed to talk to you."

"I'm here." She cut her eyes at him and shook off her confusion. "Talk"

"How do you know Carlene Stone and Nicole Gleman?"

"We came up together back in the day over in Haughville." Danesha took a step back. "Is that one of them?"

"No. No, it's neither of them."

"What's this all about then?"

Detective Jackson handed her a plastic evidence bag with a blood-stained copy of "Dust off the Ashes." Removing a pair of plastic gloves from her pocket Danesha slid them on and ripped open the evidence bag. Looking at the cover and reading Ally Love's name on the cover she knew.

"Damn." Her heart rate quickened. "What happened here, Jackson?"

"I was hoping you could tell me."

"Come again?"

"Open it to the dedication page."

She opened the book. Four names were listed in the dedication section. Her head was spinning. "Is that Ally's blood?" She sniffed the pages.

"We don't know yet but I assume it is. Just waiting 'til we get it to the lab to determine for sure if it's hers or not. Carlene Stone, Nicole Gleman, and Cheyenne Cox all crossed out in blood."

She remained silent. Her mind was a whirlwind of thoughts.

"You see the last name crossed out, Andrews?" he asked her.

"Cut the dramatics, Jackson. Am I a suspect?"

"If you were would I had called you out here and talked to you alone?"

"Hell yeah." Who was he fooling?

"Hey, I was extending a professional courtesy from one cop to another."

"Blow me, Jackson. If you have any questions for me call me through my union rep."

She shoved the book into his chest and walked off.

"If this is some sort of twisted score you're trying to settle I will find out!" he called after her.

She stopped in mid-step and headed back towards Jackson shoving her pointer finger in his chest. "Let's put it all on the table. Being concerned for my safety is a load of crap. Ally signed the damn thing to Cheyenne. She's your suspect. You're still shitty because I flipped your C-I and brought down that Mexican Cartel moving weight through Detroit."

Jackson's lip twitched. "That's crap, Andrews. Don't try to turn this thing around. You're neck-deep in this scandal and you know it. If you're not responsible you sure in the hell know who is. It's no secret you and the former Governor had it in for each other. This reeks of you and your twistiness."

Danesha laughed. "Save your conspiracy theories for the blogs. Call me when you're ready to do some real police work."

"I'm going to wipe that smug smile right off your crooked face." Jackson balled his fists up by his sides.

"Better men than yourself have tried and all failed. Believe this though, if you come after me you better finish me 'cause once you're in my cross hairs there'll be no second chances. I will end you!"

Realizing he had gotten under her skin Jackson began to laugh. "You are taking this way too personally, Andrews. I'd say a little too passionate eh? Why do you suppose that is?"

"Revenge is passion; retribution is justice. Rather revenged or avenged, when one feels wronged it's all done in passion, Jackson."

"When the fuck did you become so poetic? Tell me this then, top cop..." He smirked at her and crossed his arms with the evidence bag dangling from his right hand. "If you're not behind it aren't you just a little bit worried that there's someone out there gunning for you?"

Danesha grimaced at Jackson, removed her Louis Vuitton sunglasses from her pocket, and slipped them onto her face. It would do no good to let him see any emotion in her eyes. "Do I look worried?"

"Get the hell off of my crime scene!" Jackson was taken aback by her cockiness.

Danesha walked off swaying her ass as she moved. She did it purposely although she knew he was pissed. A man was still a man and more times than not would think with his little head before his big one, if need be that might be her ace in the hole if she ever got caught in a tight jam.

...which are you?

~Courtney Awsum

Detective Jackson maneuvered his black sedan along the winding driveway leading to the front door of the estate Ally Love once lived in. He had a meeting with her husband, Courtney Awsum. He glanced at the file in his lap as he parked. He had no idea what Courtney did for a living. From what he found through a preliminary search he had been married to the former Governor for over ten years. Graduated from college with a Master's in Business as well as in Criminal Psychology, and had never been arrested. The man had worked a number of years as a guard at the women's prison and now he held some type of position in Washington. It was a title Detective Jackson had never heard of. The file didn't even list the branch he worked for. As far as Jackson knew he could be a janitor or a clandestine spook. Jackson laughed. He doubted it was anything that dramatic, but it did raise questions in his mind. Mr. Awsum was a suspect in his wife's murder. The detective had his money on Cheyenne, but that was too cut and dry and from his experience it was usually always the spouse. The detective mentally prepared himself to be bombarded by a barrage of attorneys as soon as he stepped in the door.

He climbed out of the car still holding onto the folder, closed the car door, and approached the front door. Knocking on the door it wasn't long before it was answered by a beautiful woman who looked to be in her mid-thirties.

"Yes." The woman spoke with a British accent and looked at him questioningly.

He flashed his badge. "I'm detective Jackson. I have an appointment with Mr. Awsum."

She stepped to the side allowing him access. Once he was completely inside she closed the door. "Detective, right this way. He's expecting you."

Jackson followed her as she led him through the house and out back to the pool.

"Have a seat, Detective. He'll be out shortly." The woman unbuttoned her suit jacket.

Jackson took notice of her firearm. We'll she's no attorney, he thought as he sat with one leg crossed over the other.

"A drink, Detective?"

He considered it. Why not? "Gin and tonic."

"Straight away." Nothing else was said, she turned and was off.

He thumbed through the thin file once more. He was well aware that he may be waiting a while. It was an interrogation tactic that he often used himself before questioning a perp. He sat back and peeked over the file trying to remain inconspicuous as he attempted to figure out if Awsum was someplace nearby watching. Jackson looked up at the second-floor windows while pretending to read what was in the folder. All of the drapes were closed. He opened the file, scattered the few pages on the table beside him, and placed his hands behind his head closing his eyes. It wasn't long before the woman returned with his drink. She put it on the table beside the papers.

"He'll be with you shortly," she advised. "He's finishing a conference call."

The detective nodded and watched as the woman hurried off again. He sipped his drink. It was pleasantly warm outside. He was beginning to wish he had asked for lemonade or water instead. A few more ticks passed and he stood to his feet as a tall, fit, statuesque man approached. He wore a champagne colored silk polo shirt covered by a navy blue suede suit jacket, tan khaki's, and leather loafers. The detective took in his physical appearance concluding that he was almost seven feet and two hundred plus pounds. Awsum looked like a retired football player.

Awsum extended his hand. "Detective."

"Mr. Awsum." Jackson shook the man's hand.

Awsum pointed to the chair. "Please, Detective, have a seat."

Jackson sat obediently.

Awsum sat across from him without acknowledging the papers sprawled out on the table. He leaned back in his seat, crossed one leg over the other, folded his hands, and placed them on his knee. "Now, how can I help you?"

"First I would like to offer my condolences about your wife."

Awsum nodded. "Thank you, Detective. It's been a difficult time for us."

"I'm sure. Unfortunately, business must be attended to. Where were you on the evening of March fifth between the hours of 7:30 P.M. and 8:30 P.M?"

"I was here," Awsum answered without hesitation. "I was running late to pick her up."

"Why is that?"

Awsum stood to his feet turning his back to the detective. "I should have been there."

Jackson remained silent wondering if Awsum was trying to think of something formidable to say.

"I was here, on a business call." The man finally gave a simple response.

"With whom might I ask?"

"The Secretary of Defense."

Jackson took a sip from his glass. Was the man pulling his leg? "Can anyone confirm that?"

"Only the Secretary. I was home alone."

"Where was your daughter?"

"Excuse me?"

"Your daughter. The fact that you have a daughter is public knowledge, sir. Was she home?"

Awsum shook his head and returned to his seat. "No, she was over to a friend's."

"Is it okay for me to ask her a few questions?"

"No, it is not okay. She's only 12 years old and she's been through enough. She doesn't need to be interrogated as well."

Jackson nodded his head. "I understand. If you don't mind me asking, Mr. Awsum, what is it that you do for a living?"

"I'm a private contractor."

"Contractor?"

Awsum looked at him blankly. "Yes, sir."

"In what field?"

"I have a diverse portfolio that covers a broad range of..." Awsum shook his head and held his hands up. "I'm sorry, Detective, but what does any of this have to do with finding out who murdered my wife?"

"When investigating a case I like to get background information on those that were the closest to the deceased." Jackson didn't miss a beat.

"My line of work is very sensitive." Awsum's face expression hardened. "I feel I have told you what is applicable to your investigation regarding my whereabouts and my profession. Shall we move along? That is if you have any other questions?"

Jackson cleared his throat. "Yes sir, I do. Is there anyone you know of who might have wanted to bring harm to you or your wife?"

"She was a politician. There was no short list of those that despised and envied her. Lord forbid I speak ill of the dead, Detective, but Ally was no angel." He shrugged his shoulders and looked at the ground. "That's the nature of the beast when it comes to politics. You're going to piss people off. It just comes with the territory."

Jackson smirked. "Ahh. But the people of Indiana loved the former Governor."

Awsum looked up at Jackson. "Obviously everyone didn't or we wouldn't be having this conversation."

"Are there any possible antagonists that were angry enough to have done this? Even outside of political ties?"

"Hmm. Perhaps any radical Christian zealot against abortion or same-sex marriage."

"Any names in particular?"

"Check her website. They posted on her blog."

"She never deleted or reported any of them?"

Awsum shook his head. "She was a real politician, Detective. She could spin anything. She said the negative talk only strengthened her cause."

"Sounds like she was an extraordinary woman."

"That she was, Detective." The sadness in his voice was unmistakable. "That she was."

"Just a few more questions and I'll be out of your hair."

Awsum nodded.

"Can you tell me how close your wife was to Danesha Andrews, Carlene Stone, Nicole Gleman, and Cheyenne Cox?"

Awsum smiled. "Wow, now there are some names I haven't heard in eons. Let me see, Danesha... she and Ally had an enormous public falling out some years ago that the two never hashed out. As far as Carlene and Nicki go, Ally hadn't spoken to them in years. She used to write Cheyenne in prison, but they haven't communicated in almost twenty years. What's this all about?"

"You're sure they haven't had any contact with your wife?" Jackson's brow rose.

"None that I know of. Ally never mentioned anything to me."

"Your years as a guard over at Rockville." Jackson made a statement and looked at the dead woman's husband for reaction.

"What about them?" Awsum didn't appear unraveled.

"You were a guard at the same time that Cheyenne was there, correct?"

"Yes. And?"

"What was your interaction with her?"

"Professional. I was a guard and she was a con."

Jackson thought he saw just a hint of a twitch beneath Awsum's left eye. He continued his questioning. "You never showed any preferential treatment due to your past relationship?"

"We had no past relationship. She was Ally's friend and Ally and I weren't even dating back then."

"I see."

"Is that all, Detective?" Awsum rose from his seat once more. He'd grown tired of the probing into his family's life.

Sensing the man's discomfort, Jackson stood to shake his hand. "I apologize for the uncomfortable questions. You know chain of command... just doing my job."

Awsum ignored Jackson's motion to shake his hand. He folded his arms across his chest. "Chain of command?"

"Yes, sir. Shit rolls downhill."

"Following orders," Awsum stated.

Jackson didn't respond. He gathered the papers and placed them back into the folder.

Awsum regarded him quizzically. "In this life we are all one of two things...A puppet or a puppet master. Which are you, Detective?"

Why feed 'em at all?

~Detective Aiello

Danesha left the Bugatti parked at the shop and took her 88 Cutlass to meet up with her partner at the address in Broad Ripple. She sat outside the gate with the engine running. Rain fell down as the temperature dropped. Watching the windows begin to fog up she hit the windshield wipers and turned on the heat. Reaching into her inner suit pocket, she removed a bag of coke. Sprinkling a small amount on the back of her hand she snorted the powder. She coughed and her eyes watered. She shook her head trying to shake off the rush before pouring another nose full and snorting it. Closing the bag she placed it back in her pocket and pulled into the parking lot. She drove around the lot until she spotted Aiello's car. She sat for a few seconds before shutting off the engine and climbing out. Walking past his car, she looked through the windows and kept going. She tapped on the storage unit he said he was in. Seconds later the door rose up. Aiello stood to the side as she entered. The unit was filled from wall to wall with safes.

"Well, what do we have here?" Greed immediately poured from her eyes.

"Are we going to try to crack em all here? Or get em out of here and crack em someplace else?"

Danesha closed the door, leaned her back against it, and clasped her hands together. "If we got two, maybe three safe crackers over here how long you think it would take to crack 'em and load everything up?"

Aiello bit into his lip. "I don't know. With a subpar safecracker two maybe three hours with the amount of safes we have here. A professional, half the time."

Danesha walked over to the safe nearest to her. "Something ain't right."

"What you mean?"

"I know Nicolai is as bright as a busted light bulb but even he wouldn't leave this much cash in here like this."

So what are you saying? Just leave it?"

"Hell no. I'm just saying it's more to this."

"Like what? He's a drug dealer that's what they do. Hustle for years, stack millions and get locked up, robbed, or killed before they get to spend it."

"Maybe you're right."

Aiello laughed, jumping up and down. "Of course I'm right. How much you think is in here?"

"Your guess is as good as mine. I would feel a whole lot better about the situation if we could open these up on our own turf."

Aiello frowned. "What you mean? Turn it into evidence? All this? In here? So much of this I mean only a third will be logged. You know if we don't take it someone else in the department will. I don't know about you but I don't want to share what I worked hard for risking my life day in and day out for the past ten years. Getting shit pay for some pencil pusher to lose it in evidence lock up."

Danesha placed her hand on his shoulder. "Calm down, partner. That's not what I meant."

Aiello remained quiet. He knew she had a plan. He waited patiently as she spelled it out.

"Can't you call in a favor to your brother in law who owns the trucking company?" She looked at him hopefully.

"Yeah, I suppose. We'll have to spread a few grand around to pay him and his guys but he should keep quiet about it. Transport is covered but what about location?"

"I got a guy who does undercover work out of the South East District. I'll see if he wants a piece of the action for use of this warehouse on the lower East Side that they used last week for a sting."

"You sure about this? I mean that's a lot of people we're bringing in on this."

"It's either that or leave it. I'm not sitting around here while they try to get these things open. I don't know about you, but I don't trust some two-bit, parolee safecracker to call me up once they get all the cash out."

"I don't know. Nicolai wouldn't try anything would he? That dirtbag, weasel coward."

"You never know, he might not get heart but he might get stupid. Either way its our money now, fuck 'em and feed 'em beans."

Aiello raised an eyebrow. "Why feed 'em at all?"

***

...what do you do when you're sleeping dogs roam?

~Carlene Stone

Nicolai was already an hour overdue to drop three G packs off and pick up deposits. Pulling up on 38th and Post, he parked behind a rusted 93 Cavalier. A young Mexican guy who looked to be in his early twenties hopped out and got in the car with Nicolai. He slid Nicolai two $3,000 stacks both folded and wrapped in rubber bands. Nicolai reached underneath his seat and pulled out one of the bundles of drugs. He handed to the young man just as another got out of a Cavalier and came to Nicolai's window.

The man sitting in the car shook Nicolai's hand and got out of the car. "By the way, Nicolai, people been coming through asking 'bout you."

"Yeah? Who asking about me?"

"I don't know. People. Mr. Li Calzi's people."

"Yeah, you mean Kendricks?"

The second guy chimed in. "Nah, man. Li Calzi."

Nicolai nodded. "Thanks, I'll be sure to get in touch."

Both men stepped away from the car and Nicolai put the

Vehicle in drive. The second guy hurriedly returned to his window. "Yo, another thing."

"Yeah?" Nicolai's foot was still on the brake.

The second guy leaned over into the window, pulled his gun and started shooting into the car. Nicolai instinctively grabbed his arm and hit the gas. The man kept squeezing the trigger as he was being dragged, but none of the shots hit Nicolai as he held onto his attempted assassin and sped up. Pulling out into traffic at full speed he let go of the man's arm causing him to fall into the street in the middle of a busy roadway as Nicolai weaved in between cars.

All black Escalade pulled into the parking lot at Papa Roux's on the corner of E. 10th St. The driver hopped out and headed to the door of the restaurant. The dark tinted window of the back seat was cracked slightly only revealing the passenger's eyes.

"Get three dinners," She ordered. "Make sure they don't put no pork on my shit." She rolled the window backup and picking up her cell phone she continued her call. "Yeah, yeah. I'm here."

"Where you at?" The caller was anxious.

"The hell you mean where I'm at? I'm a grown ass woman. I'm minding my business. Where you at?"

"I'm on my way to you."

"To me? Why? We don't have no business together."

"It's about Whip."

"What about her?" The woman was not moved.

"Just meet me and bring Nicki."

"How in the hell am I supposed to find Nicole?"

"You're telling me you don't keep in touch?"

"The hell I look like? A social worker?"

"Whatever, man. Just get her and meet me at the shop in an hour."

Before she could respond, the call was ended. "This bitch is crazy." Carlene huffed as her driver climbed into the truck and placed the food on the passenger seat.

"Where to boss?" the driver asked as he started the truck.

"Where we always go every Sunday after church."

The truck pulled into traffic and Carlene sipped her Courvoisier. With her Glock resting on her lap, they headed to The Wheeler's Mission Ministries on East Michigan. It didn't take long before they were sitting outside of the mission.

"Hand me the bag," Carlene demanded as she rolled down the window. "Yo, yo, where Nicole at?" She leaned out of the window slightly.

The young girl sitting on the steps didn't answer. Had it not been for the unkempt hair and ragged clothes she could've easily passed for a model. The nine-teen-year-old beauty possessed a subtle refinement.

"You don't hear me talking to you, Niome?" Carlene was easily annoyed.

Niome stared back silently as Nicole exited the building.

Carlene's eyes reverted up to her. "Yo, Nick! I brought your favorite." Carlene held the bag out of the window.

"I told you last week and the week before that... stop coming by here."

"Just take the shit. Give it to 'ya girl if you want. We have to take a ride anyway."

"No, we don't. What can't we talk about right here?"

"Got to meet up with an old friend. She says she needs to lay some heavy info on us."

Nicole cocked her head to the side. "Old friend who? I don't have any friends."

The driver put the truck in park and climbed from the driver's seat. Nicole stepped back standing in a fighter's stance. Niome stepped next to Nicole ready to help her fight off the possible attacker. Carlene opened the door and climbed out and nodded at her driver who promptly climbed back into the truck.

Carlene walked over to Niome and placed the bag in her hands. "You look more like your mama every day." Carlene looked to Nicole and pointed to the open car door.

Nicole cut her eyes at Carlene but spoke to Niome. "Meet me at home in 'bout two hours." Reluctantly Nicole climbed into the truck.

Carlene climbed in behind her and closed the door. The driver wasted no time pulling off. Nicole avoided eye contact by staring out of her window as the three rode in silence for a moment.

"What is this all about, what's Whip up to now sitting high on her throne? I'm surprised she even has time for us lonely peasants. I swear the nerve of her." Nicole's disdain was apparent.

Carlene opened the take out box and took a bite from her Catfish Po Boy. Speech muffled as she spoke with a mouth full of food. "How long your ass going be bitter?"

Nicole turned and faced Carlene with her nose scrunched up. "What? I can't understand you."

Carlene swallowed. "I said bitter. How long your ass going be bitter about the choices you made?"

"No one's bitter."

Carlene took another bite and laughed. "You put you here. Not Whip, not me, not Danesha."

"I'm not blaming anyone. I'll get back on my feet. Don't be concerned about me."

"Um hmm...home."

"What?"

"You told that girl to meet you at home. You have a place now?"

Nicole shrugged. "I do alright."

"Uh-huh. Where y'all staying tonight?" Carlene continued to chew her food. "After we listen to this crap she tries to feed us I'll get you a room for a couple weeks."

Nicole crossed her arms. "Did I ask you to do that?"

"Naw, you ain't ask me to do that. I just told you what I was going to do."

"We don't take handouts," Nicole replied defiantly.

"Girl, please. That's all you do. What do you call going to the mission?"

"That's different."

"Yeah. Those suckers over there enable you. Come back and work."

"Work?" Nicole gaffed at Carlene's gall. "That's what you're calling it now?"

"It earns money. What would you call it?"

"Not me."

"It used to be." Carlene took another hearty bite of her sandwich.

"A long time ago," Nicole said looking out of the window again.

"You know what they say." Carlene cocked back the Glock that was sitting on her lap. "It's like riding a bike."

"Do they now?" Nicole was unfazed.

"Boss." The driver interrupted their conversation.

"Yeah?"

"We here."

Carlene looked out of the window. She hadn't even realized that the car had stopped. "Cool. Wait here. We shouldn't be here long. Keep the engine running."

Carlene and Nicole climbed from the truck and walked into the rim shop on the lower East Side. Danesha was a silent partner. She was inside waiting when the two women entered. The store was empty.

"Lock the door," Danesha ordered as she sat behind the counter counting bundles of cash. Nicole locked the door and joined the ladies at the counter.

"What's good Nick?" Danesha asked eyes still focused on the money she was counting.

"Same ole and you?"

"I'm aight."

Nicole looked around. "Where's Ally?" If this was a reunion where was everyone?

"Dead."

"Dead?" Carlene repeated unbelievingly. "I ain't seen nothing on the news or heard jack out in the streets."

"It's not being released yet. Maybe later tonight. It was someone close who hit her. Got called down by this dick I used to work with trying to feel me out."

"You're a suspect?" Nicole asked suddenly feeling on guard. "Why?"

"Whip just released a new book and dedicated it to the old crew. In the book, all of our names are crossed out in her blood."

"A hit list," Carlene stated Danesha's thought before she could express it. "On us."

Nicole let her eyes roam around the room. "What about Cheyenne? Her name on the list too?"

"Yeah."

"At least she safe, being locked up and all."

Danesha shook her head. "Not anymore."

"Why you say that?" Carlene asked thumbing her fingers through one of the bundles of cash.

Danesha eyed Carlene from the corner of her eyes then smacked her hand before answering causing Carlene to pull her hand back and flash a crooked smile. "She was released this yesterday morning."

"How come you didn't get in touch with her for the meeting?" Nicole was confused.

Danesha and Carlene eyed one another not saying anything for a second.

"You been gone from the game too long, Nick." Carlene shook her head disappointingly.

"I'ma need you to put two and two together, boo. Someone Whip knew killed her. Cheyenne just got home at the same time. All of our names are on a hit list. Damn, girl. Come on! Think."

"I don't know about this hit list thing. I ain't did nothing to nobody, least of all Cheyenne."

"You sure about that?" Carlene asked not really looking for an answer.

The three became silent. Nicole folded her arms and stared at the floor.

Danesha broke the silence. "Well, we all have our ghosts."

"What you thinking, Danesha?" Carlene hopped up on the counter.

"I say we let sleeping dogs' lie," Nicole said oblivious to the seriousness of the situation.

"Sounds good but what do you do when you're sleeping dogs roam?" Carlene asked.

Danesha and Nicole shared a flabbergasted looked then eyed Carlene.

Danesha chuckled. "What in the hell does that even mean?"

"Hell, you know what I mean. Letting our sleeping dogs lie instead of putting 'em to sleep years ago got us where we are today."

"What are you talking about, Carlene?" Nicole felt completely out of the loop.

"Nothing important," Danesha interrupted. It wouldn't do well to dredge up more dirt from the past. "I felt I owed you two a fair warning. She's gunning for us and where you take it from here is up to you. I say we work together and get her before she gets us."

"This is crazy. We're not going to hunt her down, she's our friend...was our friend."

Danesha laughed. "Bitch is you crazy? Our friend just cracked Whip's windpipe with a hardcover book."

"I don't know anything about that. Whatever the beef is, that was between Cheyenne and Whip. Count me out of this shit."

"You won't last ten minutes on the streets against Cheyenne."

"Won't have to. It won't come to that."

"Give her a piece, Carlene."

Carlene sucked her teeth. "I just have extra guns laying around in my truck right?"

"Didn't you always? I know you ain't changed that much."

Nicole interjected. "We all have. I would never 've in my worst nightmares imagined Cheyenne of all people would want any of us dead let alone be the one to put us there. Whip was a self-righteous, underhanded politician. Carlene was always hood I give her that."

Carlene smiled proudly.

Nicole continued. "But I am embarrassed when I hear some of the stories about the ruthlessness you carry out."

"Don't believe the rumors, Nick. People always talking."

"Well, the game is always the game right?"

They all hunched their shoulders.

Nicole looked at Danesha. "Danesha's a cop."

Carlene sneered. "Yeah, but she still a –G-."

"And me." Nicole's eyes filled with tears. "A homeless, on again off again alcoholic."

Danesha was over it. "Who fault is that? Don't come in here with all that crying and shit. You had the same opportunities we had. When Cheyenne went away we all split with a little under a meal ticket a piece. Should have handled it better."

Tears streamed down her face, but Nicole was convicted in her original opinion. "Let me go. Niome is waiting for me." She turned to leave.

"Wait." Danesha reached underneath the counter and removed a six shot revolver. "Take this. It's a throw away. Got six bodies on it stole it from evidence lock up so make sure you toss it when you're done."

"I told you before...I won't need it. Keep it." Nicole walked out of the store without looking back.

Danesha dropped the bundles of cash in a Louis Vuitton backpack and handed the bag to Carlene. "You know that's our last time seeing her alive right?"

...someone has to pay for the sins of the father.

~Eli

Nicolai burst through his front door with his face and neck glistening with sweat. He'd driven nonstop from Indianapolis to his home in Cleveland, Ohio. Upon entering the house, he heard music playing and smelled fresh Shawarma cooking in the kitchen. Tender bits of skewered chicken, garlic puree, and salad wrapped in pita had his house smelling wonderful. The idea of sitting and enjoying his wife's cooking would have made his stomach happy, but the fact that she was not packed and ready to go angered him. Locking the door and closing the curtains of all the windows he called out to her. "Basheera."

There was no answer.

"I know that she hears me," he mumbled to himself as he marched down the hall towards the kitchen. "Why she insists on playing these games I do not know. Basheera, why aren't you and Faizah packed and ready to go? I told you it was a matter of life and..."

As he turned the corner to the kitchen, he stopped mid-stride, he felt his stomach drop to his knees. He stuttered as he spoke. "E, e, e, Eli. What, what, what, what a surprise."

The short middle aged man sat at the kitchen table eating. Nicolai's daughter Faizah sat across from him with his wife Basheera at the stove still cooking.

"A surprise, no. This is a visit." Eli smiled while chomping into a pita. "A surprise you will not hear. A surprise is a bullet to the back of the head."

Basheera gasped as Faizah began crying.

Eli's glance switched over to Faizah. "Now, now. No need for tears, little angel. Uncle Eli's not going to hurt your father." He winked at Nicolai mockingly. "Nicolai, sit. We eat we talk."

"Eli, sir can we speak in private. Let my wife and daughter go."

"Don't make me ask again, Nicolai. Sit!"

Nicolai swallowed. He looked over at his wife then down at his daughter. He stroked Faizah's hair as he eyed the revolver sitting on the table in front of Eli. He pulled out his chair and sat.

"Basheera, the man of the house is home why is he not eating?" Eli looked over at the scared woman. "Hurry and feed him."

Basheera quickly folded the ingredients into the wrap and placed it on the table in front of her husband. She smiled at him sheepishly trying to mask her fear.

"Join us please," Eli insisted. "In my household we eat as a family. No matter what business I have in the world if I'm late for dinner with my family I answer to the real boss." Eli ran his finger across his throat as if he were being sliced with a knife. He continued with a sly grin. "My wife, or so she likes to think. Anyway, Mrs. Nicolai, sit. Eat... we talk."

Basheera did as she was told. She made herself a plate and sat next to her husband.

Eli smiled. "Now this is more like it. Tell me, Nicolai, you are Sicilian no?"

"Yes sir. On my mother's side."

"I see. Sicilian and what was your father?"

"He was Ukrainian, sir."

"No shit. Tell me how did a half Paison half Ukrainian end up with an Iraqi?" Eli asked referring to Basheera Nicolai's wife.

"Israeli."

"Come again."

Nicolai spoke through clenched teeth as veins popped out of his neck. "I said she is not Iraqi she is Israeli."

"Iraqi, Israeli...they are all the same are they not?"

Nicolai saw the look of embarrassment on his wife's face from the corner of his eyes. Avoiding eye contact, she looked down at her lap.

Eli took a bite of the pita. "Why is it that I never heard of you before today?"

"Sir?"

"Your name. I never heard your name before today. My storage facility was hit. I asked the right people the right questions and all I heard was Nicolai Gaponenko, Nicolai Gaponenko. And I'm thinking and thinking but I don't know any Nicolai. Why should he know me and know about my personal business? You have an answer to that for me, Nicolai Gaponenko?"

"Kendricks."

"Kendricks... He tells me, after much back and forth, that it was you."

"Kendricks, sir... He is lying. I...."

"Nicolai, do you know how you can tell if a man is lying?"

Nicolai shook his head no. Eli swung his head around as he heard the front door being kicked in and footsteps marching towards his direction. Jumping from his seat, he stood behind Nicolai's wife and daughter wrapping his arms around them. Nicolai stood and removed a straight razor from his jacket pocket. Basheera gasped as Nicolai and his daughter both cried. Within seconds, his kitchen was filled with men dousing the room with gasoline. One of his men placed a white blood stained handkerchief on the table in front of Basheera.

Eli unwrapped the handkerchief. "Every man is different. The amount of pain one man can sustain compared to another varies from man to man. Overall, pain brings out the truth sooner or later. With some, just the flashing of a knife is enough to bring the truth out of them. With others, you have to take a finger or two. Then there's the hard case types. The die-hard loyal cocksuckers like Kendricks. Why he would be loyal to a piece of shit like you is beyond me. But his type..." He paused for dramatics and snatched the handkerchief from the table revealing a severed hand.

Nicolai spit up getting the majority of his vomit on his wife's chest.

Eli merely chuckled. "Stubborn, want to be tough shits like that got damned Kendricks you have to take the whole hand before you can erase the lies." He stared at Nicolai with disgust. "Israeli or not you don't deserve a woman. A weak stomach? You are not the man of the house. This little girl and woman have more balls than you."

"Please, just let us go. I promise we will not say anything!" Basheera screamed out as tears streamed from her face. "Nicolai, just tell him what he wants to know!"

"Ssh, ssh, ssh." Eli, now eye to eye with Basheera, whispered to the woman. "It is too late. Someone has to pay for the sins of the father." Grasping her arm he slammed it down on the table with her palm flat.

Nicolai moved to her defense but was punched in the eye by one of Eli's men. He hit the floor clutching his eye. Basheera squirmed as Eli tightened his grip. She swung with her free hand.

The man that punched Nicolai placed a gun to the back of his daughter's head and stared at Basheera pointedly. "Be still or he will blow your little girl's head off."

Basheera stopped squirming. Nicolai looked up from the floor defenseless as his wife and daughter were at the mercy of these men.

"I want to know where my product is and I want the truth. Every time I feel like you are telling me anything other than the truth..." Eli placed the blade on Basheera's pinky finger and applied pressure.

The frail woman screamed out as she felt the blade slice through her finger.

Eli glared at Nicolai. "I will take a finger. Thought I would take one to start off with... just for good measure."

Nicolai jumped to his feet screaming. The gunman moved the gun from his daughter's head to his chest stopping mid stride. His eye fell upon his sobbing wife. "I'm sorry baby. I'm so sorry for bringing this into our home."

Basheera clutched her bloody hand. Screaming in disbelief, she stared at the finger that was once attached to her hand now lying on the table looking like a Vienna sausage.

"I'll tell you!" Nicolai screamed out as his body involuntarily shivered in fear. "Whatever you want to know I'll tell you!"

Hmm...the proof is in the blood.

~Detective Jackson

Nicole got off of the bus on the corner of Sherman and Washington Street. The neighborhood was littered with trash and prostitutes. Pausing down the street from where she lived she removed the Obama phone she had in her pocket. That's what they called the government assisted free cell phones. Searching through the phone book, she found the name she was looking for. Black Love, she pressed the talk button and waited patiently as it rang. After four rings when she thought the answering machine would come in a voice chimed through the other end.

"Hello, Black....Black Love you don't know me this is Whip's friend. Well, we aren't friends anymore we used to be. Anyway she told me if I ever get in a jam and need help legal or otherwise I could count on you. I'm calling to tell you your sister is dead you need to get out here some serious stuff is about to go down."

The other end of the line was silent. She spoke again.

"Hello, are you there?"

"Yes, yes I'm here. What happened to Ally?"

"Not sure can explain more once you get here."

"That's going to take some time, in Nigeria, on sort of a job."

"I'm about to run out of minutes try to call me back once you get here, get here as soon as you can." She pressed the end button on the phone and dropped it in her pocket. Continuing home she nodded at the old man who took care of the building she was renting the room out of. Making her way through the exterior door she climbed the three flights of stairs to the level her room was on. Walking down the hall she heard the old mildewed carpet squish underneath her feet. The wet carpet smell was drowned out by the smell of chicken being burned in fish grease coming from one of the rooms. From the corner of her eye, she saw a mouse scamper across the hall from underneath someone's room door then quickly squeezing underneath another door. Pulling the single key from her bra, she slid it in the lock, turned it, and twisted the door knob. She walked inside and hurriedly closed the door behind her.

"What's good, Nick?" Cheyenne asked laid out across the bed.

Nicole didn't answer. Her eyes roamed the small room.

"You expecting someone, Nick?"

Nicole was worried about Niome. Had Cheyenne killed her and stuffed her in the closet? She inched towards the worn door of her only closet. Cheyenne, laying with her arms behind her head and hands situated underneath a pillow, sat up folding her legs Indian style. From under the pillow she pulled out an eight inch jagged blade and laid it on her lap.

"Cheyenne, please," Nicole said rolling her eyes unimpressed with the method of intimidation her old chum had chosen. "I been cut before."

"Not as deep as I've been cut."

"Yeah, well emotional wounds hurt the most don't they?"

"Hurt like a bitch." Cheyenne rose from the mattress and stood by the bed.

"Don't help much either when you pulling the scabs off."

"Well, guess I'm just a gluten for pain."

Nicole reached for the closet door.

"What you looking for, Nick?"

Nicole felt goose bumps on the back of her neck. As she ignored Cheyenne, she snatched the door open. All of her clothes were on the closet floor.

"Yeah, I checked already. Sorry about the mess, I was never a thief. Didn't have the heart to take what someone else worked for. Your stash of $150.00 is still there. No guns or knives. I was asking about you when I was in. Heard you were a lush. I ain't believe it. I mean the old Nick from back in the day kept two hammers."

Relieved that Niome wasn't there Nicole let out a sigh. She turned to face Cheyenne. "That was back in the day." Nicole launched at Cheyenne impulsively but Cheyenne stepped to the side dodging her attack. Off balance, Nicole fell face first catching herself with her hands on the dresser near the bed.

Cheyenne laughed as Nicole kicked back with her left foot pushing her into the crouch. Cheyenne hunched over as she felt a sharp pain shoot to her stomach. Shaking it off, she grabbed Nicole by the back of her hair. Pulling her towards her Cheyenne wrapped her arm around her throat cutting off her oxygen and choking her from behind. Nicole squirmed and threw elbows. With her arms flailing, she managed to grab one of Cheyenne's ears. Clutching tight, she snatched the yellow diamond from her ear. Cheyenne squealed as she felt blood running down the side of her face. She tightened her grip around Nicole's neck and shoved the jagged knife into her sternum. She heard the bone crack as she pulled the knife upwards. She felt it the moment Nicole's legs went limp and instantly dropped her body. Looking down at her old friend she knelt down beside her body to retrieve the earring that Nicole was still clutching. A tap on the door startled her.

"Nicole," the voice from the other side of the door called out.

Cheyenne remained silent.

The female visitor knocked again. "I'm selling plates if you and your girl want to get one."

Cheyenne heard the woman grab the door handle. Leaving the earring and the knife she hurried to her feet and made her way to the window leaving the way she had got in. She climbed back up to the roof and trotted across the rooftop to the rear of the building where she effortlessly climbed down. As she reached the ground and turned the corner, she spotted Carlene standing on the porch talking to the old man. Turning to go in the other direction, she bumped into Niome.

"Watch where the fuck you going little girl," Cheyenne spat out as she kept walking.

"Fuck you too," Niome mumbled as she continued on her way. Walking up the stairs to the porch, she spotted Carlene pulling away. "What did she want?" Niome asked the old man.

"Looking for your mother. You know I told her no guests beyond the porch."

Niome folded her arms and rocked back and forward from one leg to the next. She eyed the six pack of Red Bull underneath his chair on the porch. "You sure she didn't go up there?"

"You calling me a liar?"

Niome inhaled impatiently. "What she give you a six pack for?"

"None of your damn business, missy."

Niome knew he was lying but had no way to actually prove it and arguing with him would get her nothing but a headache. She walked off into the building as he continued to rant and swear. Taking her trek up the stairs and down the hall she finally made her way to the room and unlocked the door. Twisting the doorknob and pushing the door open she walked into the room. It only took a second for her eyes to fall upon the body. She felt her knees get weak and stomach turn queasy. "Mama..." She slowly walked over to her mother lying on the floor and shook her frantically. "Get up, mama."

Her dead body still felt warm. Her blood oozed onto the floor and all over Niome. Niome cradled her mother's head. She stared down into her dead brown eyes that stared back at her lifeless. Niome felt a chill rush through her as she wiped the tears from her face smearing her mother's blood across her cheeks. She let Nicole's head rest in her lap as she kissed her forehead, her left hand, and then her right. With tears in her eyes, she felt the stickiness of blood on her lips as she looked closer at her mother's clenched fist. She pried it open and removed the bloody yellow diamond. She gently laid Nicole's head back on the ground and got on her knees hunched over her mother's lifeless frame. "I love you, mama. Don't worry. I'll do the right thing."

She gripped the knife with both hands and ripped it from her mother's chest. Blood squirted into the air splattering her face and the walls behind her. Standing to her feet, she wiped the bloody knife clean on the bed spread. Tucking the knife into the front of her pants, she went to the closet and quickly changed clothes. Next opening the envelope that was lying on the pile of clothes on the floor she took the $150.00 dollars and ran down the hall, down the stairs and out of the building. Rushing towards the old man in the chair as he popped the cap on a can of his Red Bull beer she clamped her left hand around his throat knocking him out of his chair. Before he could respond, she had the pointy end of the blade underneath his eye.

"I'm giving you one chance, old man, to convince me that you did not let that bitch into our room." She felt the warmth from his pants soak through staining her pants as he pissed himself out of fear.

"I swear to Christ I did not let her or anyone else up those steps." Tears streamed from his eyes.

Niome didn't believe him, but she didn't have the heart to kill him. Carlene, on the other hand, was another story. She took the butt of the knife and let it fall down on his face knocking his front teeth out. In doing so, she broke the skin on her fingers causing a light trickle of blood to run down the handle of the knife. She stood over him as he clutched his bloody mouth crying. The other residents watched in fear as she hopped off the porch and ran down the block.

Niome roamed the streets for hours with no place to go and no one to turn to. All the family she had in the world was dead. It wasn't long before her stomach began to growl. It was three in the morning and nothing was open. She found herself on the West Side. The only people on the street at this hour were drug addicts and prostitutes. Every so often a police cruiser would roll pass. The temperature dropped as the rain began to drizzle. It didn't take long before she found herself caught in a down pour. It was raining so hard she could hardly see in front of her. Ducking underneath a viaduct, she stood there until the storm cleared. Four hours had passed before the sun was beginning to come up. She made her way to a McDonald's and ordered hot cakes, sausage, and orange juice. She set her food on the table and went into the restroom where she washed her face in the sink she then hurried back to her food. Taking her time eating she let a plan of revenge form in her mind. It was simple she thought. Find Carlene, kill her, and get out of town.

One hour later she was getting off of the bus a block away from the chop shop Carlene ran on the lower East Side. Walking towards the auto shop Carlene used as a front she kept her head down. Stopping two doors down she had a perfect view of everyone that came in and out. Pulling twenty dollars from her pocket, she approached a homeless woman camped out underneath a blanket. "Twenty bucks for the cart and blanket."

"Piss off," the old lady spit out as she rolled over, turning her back to Niome.

Niome pulled out another five dollar bill. "Twenty-five and you can keep the cart."

The old woman stood up. "Cash first."

Niome held the money in the air. The old lady tried to snatch it as Niome pulled her hand back. "Carlene Stone, the woman owns this place. You see her this morning?"

"What business is it of yours?"

"You want the cash or not?"

"She don't never get here this early. She'll be by afternoon."

Niome shoved the money into her hand. "Beat it."

The woman shoved the money into her pocket, grabbed her cart, and shuffled down the street. Niome picked up the blanket, wrapped herself in it, and laid on the ground with her eyes focused on the entrance to the chop shop.

***

Detective Jackson had a busy morning. He had just gotten back to the city from the Rockville Correctional Facility for women in Rockville, IN. Before he had a chance to process the information, he'd just learned he was called in to the murder scene of Nicole Gleman. He hummed "Sara" by Hall and Oates as he walked down the hall on his way to see the Medical Examiner. Clutching a box of Dunkin Donuts, he pushed the stainless steel doors open to the county morgue. Walking pass lifeless bodies underneath sheets on stainless steel tables he stopped once reaching the M.E. "You get my body yet?" He asked as he lifted the top to the box offering her one of the donuts.

She reached into the box removing a powdered, jelly filled donut. "Over here." She took a bite of the donut and led the way to the table with Nicole's body on it. She pulled the sheet back and stood back as he approached the table eyeing the slashed remains.

"Tell me about it." He closed the box and set it on a nearby table.

"A jagged sharp instrument was used. You see the tear marks in the flesh from here to here? It sort of ripped the flesh like a pair of shears. She was stabbed once in her mid- to upper-left torso...right here in the middle of her chest... from behind."

"How do you know it was from behind?"

The M.E. held her donut with her hand while pointing at Nicole's neck with her pinky finger. "You see the indentation around her throat?"

Detective Jackson leaned in closer for a better view.

Stuffing the remainder of the donut in her mouth the medical examiner pressed gently on the victim's neck. "Feel here. The trachea and isthmus of the thyroid gland are smashed in signifying that it was being suppressed, hence the marks on her neck. The laceration to her chest was one-eighth of an inch deep. She died instantly. There were also superficial cuts and bruises on her hands."

"Any chance any of this blood has our killer's DNA blended with it?"

"As a matter of fact yes."

Detective Jackson looked surprised as he flashed a coffee-stained smile.

She motioned for him to come closer as she picked up a cotton Q-tip and pointed at the corpse's open hand. A small fragment of drying blood sat in the center of her palm. The medical examiner scraped the blood with the Q-tip, dropped it in a tube, and sealed it. "I'll run some tests and let you know but I'm pretty sure it could be the attacker. Looks like this sample is from a self-defense wound. Look at her knees. Fresh scars. She definitely put up a fight. Any suspects yet?"

"One... Maybe two. The last to see her alive was her daughter."

"Daughter? Hmm."

"Hmm, what?"

"Unless she adopted a child this woman didn't have any children."

"How can you be so sure?"

"Because this woman has never had intercourse. Well, at least not vaginally."

"She has to be almost forty and you're telling me she's a virgin?"

"It's typical in cases like this that I do a rape kit. The tests came back negative for semen or vaginal tears."

"Yeah and?"

"The old school way of doing things would have been to observe the hymen, the tissue that stretches across the interior opening into the vagina. Generally, if the tissue is intact you're a virgin. If the tissue is ripped or absent, then you are not a virgin. At least, that's the old-school way of looking at it. In the modern times, it's not so simple."

"Why not, doc?"

"Modern medicine has proven that the hymen can be broken in many different ways without actually having engaged in sexual intercourse. Women have different shapes and sizes of vaginas so whereas one woman who may not be a virgin may still have her hymen intact another woman, or girl, who has not had sex may have broken hers from walking or playing sports. There really is no medical way to tell other than to ask the woman."

"Old school or not what is your professional opinion?"

"I say she never had sex. The hymen does typically break before a woman reaches her forties."

"How does this hymen thing work again?"

"It's simple. When it's ripped or broken there is a thin film of blood, what some cultures in Africa call the proof of blood. It's when the husband takes his bride for the first time."

"A real life Virgin Mary here," Jackson stated in awe. "Hmmm. The proof is in the blood."

...your sense of honor or your sense of financial security?

~Eli

Twelve safes in all, four safe crackers, Danesha, and Aiello were all situated in a warehouse on the East Side. On the floor sat thirty duffle bags and no cash. Danesha and Aiello stared at the bags they'd stuffed. Both remained silent for several moments lost in their own thoughts.

Aiello broke the silence. "How are we going to move all this undetected? A few ounces here and there is cool. But this... this? Someone's going to be looking for this."

Danesha remained silent as she began loading half the bags in the back of her Tahoe.

"Are you not hearing me?" He asked as he paid the safe crackers.

"We in it now," Danesha commented leaving the other bags on the ground near Aiello's truck.

"In what now? Hold that thought." He turned to their safecrackers. "You four beat it. And I don't have to tell you..."

"Hey! Whatever the hell it is I don't want to be a part of it," one of the men stated holding his hands in the air. "If anything don't you two tell anyone we were the ones who opened these for you."

"Scram." Aiello barked the order as he slid the warehouse door open and the four men scuffled through it. As he slammed the door closed, he heard the engine to Danesha's Tahoe turn over. Walking over to the truck, he leaned his head through the window. "Hold on we need to talk about this."

"About what, Aiello?"

"Someone's going to be looking for this." He repeated his concern and looked at her with a serious glare.

"Sit on it until I say it's safe to unload it."

"Unload it to who? Once it hit the streets the owners are going to..."

"Just sit on it! Let's move. I have other business."

He walked over to the door and slid it open before stepping to the side to watch as she pulled out. Quickly tossing the bags in the back of his truck he hopped in and pulled off. Smoking Marlboro after Marlboro, he found himself sitting outside his brother in law's house in the driveway. He called him from the truck. "Manny, it's me. Open the garage." He ended the call and a few minutes later the garage door opened allowing him to pull in. He climbed out of the truck.

"What's going on?" Manny asked looking worried.

"I need a drink." Aiello attempted to pass Manny to go inside the house.

Manny grabbed him by the arm and pulled him back. "What's the deal, bro?"

"I... I need to keep this here for a few days."

"Hold on what are you talking about?" Manny's eyebrow rose. "Keep what here?"

"You know." He nodded towards the vehicle. "The truck."

"Why? What's in the truck?"

Aiello ran his hand through his hair. "Can you just do this one thing for me without taking me through all this hoopla?"

"What are you hiding?" He waited for a response and when he saw that one was not forthcoming, he threw up his hands. "You know what? Fine. Get that thing out of here before your sister sees it and starts asking questions I don't even want to know what you have in there. Just get it the hell off my property."

"Hold on, damn." Aiello walked to the rear of the truck and opened the door. Sliding a bag over he unzipped it slowly and motioned for Manny to take a look.

Manny peered into the bag. "Is that what I think it is?"

"A shitload of Heroin."

"No." Manny was astonished.

"Just for a few days, man. I don't have any other place to go."

"Jesus... how much do you think is in here?"

"I don't know. Wholesale, two. Two and a half maybe."

"Million?"

Aiello nodded. "Yeah."

"Dollars?" Manny dropped to his knees. "We're going to die. We're all going to die."

"For Christ's sake get off the ground." Aiello zipped up the bag, shook his head, and shut the door.

"They are going to hunt us down and kill us."

"No one's going to die as long as you keep your mouth shut and keep Marie out of our business."

"Two and a half million dollars." Manny held his head in his hands and shook it from side to side. "Man, you get two days."

Aiello helped his brother-in-law to his feet. "I need at least two weeks, Manny."

"Can't do it. I would be putting my family in danger. I ain't gotta tell you that."

"Give me a week then."

Manny sighed reluctantly. "A week."

"Yes. Thank you, man. I mean..."

"A week for fifty percent," Manny stated staring Aiello dead in the eyes.

Aiello was appalled. "I'm not giving you a million dollars for a week's storage."

Manny motioned to the garage door with his thumb. "Back it on out of here then."

"Two-fifty." Aiello needed to bargain his way out of giving over half his cut.

Manny nodded and held up his index finger. "One week! After that, I drive this thing out of here myself and leave it somewhere."

"Deal." Manny was relieved that the crisis was averted. "Can I get that drink now?"

Niome eyed the car repair shop without blinking. She had been lying on the cold ground for more than three hours. The wind whistled around her, but the elements didn't bother her. She was used to it. She'd spent the majority of her life on the streets. She was right at home in this environment. She would wait all night if she had to. Niome felt her nerves become anxious every time a car pulled up and parked in front of the business. She knew she would only get one shot at this so she had to make it work.

She watched as a postal delivery truck parked in front of her. She couldn't help but stare at the woman sitting behind the wheel. She knew she didn't know the woman, but there was something oddly familiar about her. Niome tried to look elsewhere, but she couldn't. It was as if she were drawn to the stranger. The female postal worker got out of the truck wearing a postal uniform that was obviously too big for her. She winked at Niome before grabbing the bag of mail and crossing the street. Niome looked inside the truck and saw stacks of envelopes and boxes scattered all over the seats and floor. Looking back up to see if the woman was looking, she moved in to get a closer look. She saw blood on some of the envelopes and the steering wheel. Niome stepped away from the truck and watched. The woman continued walked with her head held low looking through envelopes. She approached the car repair shop and walked in. Niome stood with her back against the fence and waited.

Mentally she did a quick run through of past scenarios from the previous 48 hours hoping she could conjure up a memory of where she knew this mail lady from. The sound of music speakers rattling from an approaching vehicle brought her back to the here and now. Niome eyed Carlene's truck as it stopped at the light down the block from the repair shop. She tapped the butt of the knife she had tucked under her shirt to make sure it was secured. The blanket was wrapped around her as she began to step forward. The light turned green and the truck accelerated. With one foot on the curb and one foot in the street, she paused. Feeling a shortness of breath she took a step back onto the sidewalk. She ducked as she heard four loud pops come from inside the car repair shop.

Carlene's truck zipped down the block screeching to a dead stop in the middle of the street. Without warning three cars swarmed. The rear door to Carlene's truck swung open. Niome held her breath as she contemplated rushing the truck and jabbing Carlene as soon as she stuck her head out of the truck. The door to the car repair shop burst open as the woman wearing the postal uniform came out blasting. The first shot hit Carlene's driver in the forehead as he stepped from the rear of the truck. He crumbled to the ground as the assassin stepped forward and kept firing. The men from the three cars jumped out returning fire forcing the lone gun-woman to fight her way to safety. She didn't hesitate as she moved towards her mail truck. The rat, a tat, tat, tat of the A-K 12 echoed through the streets. As they realized, they were outgunned they took cover.

She kept firing as she moved across the street. Each step was more livelily than the last. Almost to her getaway vehicle bullets whizzed by her feet. For one last hurrah she turned to spray her adversaries with a grin and an extended clip. With a quick spin in the direction that the firing was coming from the chopper, was ready to go to work again. One hand almost on the truck, she was pushed back by a bullet that hit her in the side. The lone assassin dropped to one knee, lowered her gun, and clutched her side. She looked down at her hand seeing that her fingers were wet. A chuckle escaped her lips. There was a faint touch on her shoulder that caused her to whip around to face the threat. The nozzle of the barrel met face to face with Niome sitting behind the wheel of the postal truck. The young girl gasped as she threw her hands in the air.

"Don't shoot!" Niome screamed out as she wrestled with herself about who she should be paying more attention to: this crazy postal worker with a gun in her face or a bevy of thugs rushing across the street firing in their direction.

The gunman saw the mob and made the decision for her. "Start driving, kid!"

Niome shifted into drive and pulled off as the postal worker jumped in with the upper part of her body lying across Niome and her legs hanging from the truck. Niome wrestled with the wheel to keep control of the vehicle as the assassin struggled to get across her lap and into the passenger seat. Niome slowed down as the woman got situated. A tink, tink, tink sound occurred as a result of metal piercing metal as gunshots flew from behind them. The assassin, now in her seat, slouched low gripping her AK-12.

"Why are you slowing down?" She was regretting her decision to seek help from the stranger.

"I thought it would be easier for you to get situated and..."

"Forget it kid, just stop."

Niome kept her eyes focused on the road. "Stop what? Talking?"

"No, the truck. Stop the truck!"

Niome didn't understand her reasoning nevertheless she did as she was told slamming on the brakes. Niome watched from the corner of her eye as she ducked her head between her legs as her new found accomplice jumped up and took aim. She squeezed as one of the cars chasing them tried to swerve out of the way. It was too late. They veered into a school bus full of children. The postal worker stepped from the truck still firing turning the car and everyone in it into confetti. The other two cars reversed their vehicles fleeing the scene as the sound of sirens invaded the air. She walked back to the truck and climbed in.

Niome shifted into drive and hit the gas. The little truck jerked forward leaving behind twisted metal and carnage. Heading down Washington Street, she drove as fast as the small truck would carry them veering onto the highway. The woman leaned back with her gun pointed at Niome. She gave her directions on where to go to next.

Niome remained silent driving the way the woman instructed. She got off at an exit near downtown, drove a few blocks, and pulled into an underground parking garage at a condo complex.

"Turn the engine off."

Niome did as she was told and dropped her hands to her side.

"Keep your hands on the wheel."

Niome put her hands back on the steering wheel.

"Who the hell are you?"

Niome kept her eyes focused out the window. "Is she dead?"

"This is the last time I'm asking. Who are you?"

"Just tell me... Is she dead?"

The woman pressed the barrel of the gun against Niome's forehead. Niome didn't flinch or waver she stared back with tears wetting her face. The woman let the weapon fall to her lap. "No she's not dead."

Niome heaved heavily as she banged on the steering wheel. "What do you mean she's not dead? I heard."

"It was a setup, kid. They were waiting for me." She gasped as she clutched her side. Blood seeped through her fingers. "Get out."

"You're hurt. I can help."

She tried to lift the gun once more but dropped it on the side of the seat. Beads of sweat popped up on her forehead. "I said get the hell out of here."

Niome tried to reason with her. "She killed my mother."

"People die every day all day. It's unfortunate. It's life. Now get out."

"I want her dead just as much as you do. Let me help you. Maybe we can get her together."

She laughed then coughed from the pain.

Niome continued to reason. "I saved your life back there. That has to count for something. You owe me."

"The hell I do. Move on. You'll get us both killed. You're not even a good get away driver. How the hell do you expect to walk up to someone in broad daylight, put a gun in their mouth, pull the trigger, and walk off like you're taking a Sunday stroll without getting yourself shot or busted?"

"You can teach me. I can be an asset."

"This ain't some college course you take over at Ivy Tech. You learn on the job. If you fail this course ain't no re-takes."

"Don't worry about me. I can hold my own."

"It ain't you I'm worried about, little girl. If you screw up we're both dead."

"I'm begging you... I can help you. Please let me help you."

Niome reached out towards her wound and the woman smacked her hand away. "The hell wrong with you? Don't put your dirty hands near my wound."

"I'm sorry. I just want to—"

"Help." The woman finished her sentence for her. "Yeah, I know. Tell me why I should let you help me."

"Haven't you ever done anything for someone just because?"

"Hell naw."

"Well, I have. I did just an hour ago."

"No one asked you to, dumbass. Risk your life for me! Umph. I ain't ask you to do that shit. Did I?"

Niome turned her head and folded her arms across her chest.

"Did I?" The gunman's voice echoed through the empty parking garage.

Niome jumped as she felt a chill run up her spine. Niome turned and faced her with her nose flared, eyes narrowed, and one eyebrow raised. "No, you didn't. You didn't have to. I did it 'cause it was the right thing to do."

"I need a better reason than that."

"I told you she killed my mother."

"No, you could've called the cops. Don't feed me that, tell me why you want to do this."

"Knowing that she is still alive and I did nothing, I mean nothing, to avenge my mother's death would hollow me inside. I would never rest. I could never live with myself. You might not know what it's like to lose someone you love, but I do. I might as well be dead too."

"I know kid." She said barely audible.

"What?"

"I said give me a name, kid?"

Niome paused.

"You came to me remember." The woman looked at her quizzically.

"Niome."

"Niome?"

"Yeah."

"The first time I tell you to do something and you don't, this arrangement is over and it may not end the way you want it to."

Niome nodded.

"However it ends I'll deal with it."

***

Manny spent the majority of his day in his office at his desk drinking coffee and chasing it with Martel. He hadn't slept all night thinking about what he had in the garage. Not to mention the arguing he had to do with his wife about why she wasn't allowed to go into the garage. The nerve of his brother-in-law. He had the right mind to drive it a few blocks over and leave it. He lived in a beautiful home, owned a profitable business, and a great wife and kids. Why should he risk all of that to do this favor for his selfish brother- in-law on top of all the other illegal favors he'd done for him? Manny sighed. I can do this, he thought. One week in exchange for two hundred grand. He rose from his desk and went to the break room. Standing by the microwave talking were two of his employees, John, his foreman, and Osama a Middle Eastern man who had only been in the company for a few days.

Manny walked over to the coffee pot to brew a fresh pot. "Hey, Osama. Can I get a word with you alone?"

"Sure boss." The man grabbed his coffee mug from a nearby table, waited for his boss to finish his task, and then followed Manny back to his office.

Manny closed the door behind them.

"What's up boss?" Osama looked concerned.

"Have a seat, please."

Osama sat, taking a sip from his cup. "What's this all about, sir?"

"I want to ask you something and I don't want you to take this the wrong way."

"I'll try not to. What's on your mind?"

"If I remember correctly you were recently paroled from prison for narcotics distribution."

Osama stood to his feet. "Is that a question?"

Manny held his hands up motioning for Osama to sit back down.

Osama shook his head. "I prefer to stand thank you."

"It's not what you think."

"That life is behind me I..."

"Osama how would you like to make twenty-five thousand dollars?"

Osama remained silent.

Manny walked around his desk, reached into his bottom drawer and removed his bottle of Martel. Walking back over to Osama, he removed the top and poured a shot into Osama's cup. "Go ahead. Drink it."

Osama took a full gulp and gasped.

Manny sat on the edge of his desk. "Is it safe to assume that some of your old associates from back in the day, you can... uh... get in touch with them if need be?"

Osama nodded. "I still know a few guys."

"I recently came across some product only I don't have a distributor."

Osama's eyebrow rose. "Came across it how?"

"Came across it, came across it. What do you care?"

Osama shrugged. "I'm sorry. I'm just asking. If I get a cut for introducing you to a guy and my cut is that big you must have some major weight. My associates are going to ask the same thing."

"Let me worry about that when that comes up. Can you get me in a room with the right people or not?"

"I don't know. They don't like meeting new people. Maybe if you give me the stuff and I make the deal for you."

Manny shook his head no. "Not going to happen. I have a partner who asked to remain anonymous, but it goes without saying he would be against that idea."

"Let's say I do get you a meet... what kind of product are you even talking about?"

"What does it matter?" He leaned in closer and whispered. "A drug dealer's a drug dealer. They should be able to sell anything."

Osama regained moxie. "Look man you came to me. I'm not going to my guy and not have anything to tell him." He turned to walk out of the office.

Manny grabbed his arm to stop him. He sighed. "Heroin. A lot of heroin."

"How do I know the stuff's any good?"

"Can you get me with the guy or what?"

Osama considered it. "I'll see what I can do."

Manny released his arm and nodded his head.

Osama was feeling a little leery about the situation. "And boss... let's keep this between us alright?"

Manny nodded once more and Osama walked out of his office.

***

Carlene drank peach flavored Ciroc out of the bottle as she paced the area of her living room. She had to use a cane to balance herself. Cheyenne had shot her in the leg during their shoot out. Her bulletproof vest was open and two guns were swinging from holsters on both sides of her. Lieutenants and soldiers from her team occupied the room waiting to see what would be done next. Setting the bottle on the dining room table, she picked up an APS urban assault rifle from the table and cocked it back. "I can't believe you bitch ass Niggas let her get away!"

Everyone remained silent.

She walked around the room looking into the eyes of all the men there. "Nothing to say?" She shook her head in disbelief. "What am I paying y'all for?"

"We'll get her boss," a young soldier said. He couldn't have been older than nineteen years old.

She paused and took a step back coming eye to eye with the young boy. "What was that?"

"I said we'll get her." His mumbling was barely audible.

She smashed the butt of her gun into his face and he dropped to his knees clutching his bloody nose and mouth. "And just how are we going to do that?" she asked staring down at him.

He remained on his knees not responding.

"Come on. It was your suggestion, right? We going to get her boss. Ain't that what you said? Tell me, since you're the brains of this operation now, how you plan to get her and you don't even have a clue as to where to start looking."

"I was just..."

Cocking the gun back and aiming at his head, she glared at him. "You better make it good."

"I..." He dropped his head.

She laughed. "Best damn thing you said all morning." Walking back to the table and retrieving her bottle of liquor, she took a swig and sneered at her group. "I want eyes and ears everywhere. Pay motherfuckers, beat 'em up, threaten to kill the people they love... I don't care. Every fiend, pusher, and hooker. Every little kid that run these streets, restaurants, bars, and hotels... Somebody saw her ass. Check the hospitals and pharmacies. I hit her. Don't know if it was fatal but a bullet's a bullet. She's somewhere in this city bleeding. Somebody saw that shit. Find out who it is and we find her."

***

Niome waited until dark then climbed into the mail truck and drove it to the other side of town. It was risky, but she took the highway knowing it would be quicker. Getting off at exit 35 in Castleton, she drove a few blocks from Castleton mall and parked it. Getting out she took a better part of twenty minutes wiping down the steering wheel and dashboard, the doors and outside of the truck. Looking over the truck once more to see if there was a spot she may have missed she opened the door and wiped down the gear stick. Pulling the knife from her pants, she wiped it down and left it in the truck on the seat. She closed the door, wiped it down once more, and walked until she found a cab to take her back to her partner.

***

She had a lot of questions she wanted to ask her. Why she wanted Carlene dead, did she kill the postal driver that was driving the mail truck, and how could she afford the condo they were hiding out in? She thought better of springing the questions upon her considering that the relationship between the two of them was strange enough and way too new. She didn't want to add any undue pressure to the situation by asking too many questions. Niome used the electronic key her partner gave her to let herself into the parking garage then took the stairs up to the condo they were staying in. Unlocking the door she entered quickly.

"I'm back!" She yelled out after looking around and seeing that the woman was nowhere in sight. She walked down the hall to the bathroom and saw that the door was slightly cracked. She pushed it open to get a better view. The woman was laying in the tub with a tray next to her with alcohol and medical gauze. A hemostat was in her hand. She simply refused to go to the hospital. Niome watched as she tried to remove the bullet on her own. Blood began to taint the water in the tub leaving light strands of red floating about it. In Niome's mind, it almost looked like art. She smiled.

The woman looked up and rolled her eyes in frustration. "Glad to see you don't have a weak stomach. Wash your hands then get over here and help me."

Niome did as she was told washing her hands thoroughly and scrubbing them up to her elbows. After drying them, she moved the tray to the side so that she could get access to the wound. Taking the hemostats from the woman's hand she also picked up some gauze and sopped up as much blood as she could from the opening.

"You ready?" Niome looked into her eyes.

She nodded yes as she gripped the tub. Niome dug into the hole in her side feeling around for the bullet that launched into her. The woman groaned eerily as she gripped Niome's arm in pain trying to get her to stop.

"You have to let go," Niome explained. "Let me do this. If I don't get it out you're going to die."

The woman's sweat drenched face glistened as tears escaped her eyes and trickled down her face dripping from her chin to her chest. She slowly let go of Niome's arm turning her head so that she couldn't look at it. She cried hysterically as Niome poked and probed. After ten minutes of teeth-shattering pain Niome felt the hemostats grip something. She closed her eyes and prayed it wasn't a piece of tissue or a vital organ. She wasn't a doctor and she had no idea what she was doing. She took a deep breath and pulled. Her partner's body jumped as blood started oozing from the wound.

"I got it!" Niome exclaimed as she dropped the bloody hemostats and the bullet on the floor. She quickly pulled the drain in the tub and doused the wound with rubbing alcohol. She expected to hear the woman yell out in pain, but she was uncannily quiet. Niome paused and looked over at her. She felt her nerves kick in. The woman wasn't moving. Her first thought was that she killed her during her haste to save her life. Niome tensely checked her pulse. Thank God, she's still breathing, Niome thought as she dried the wound the best she could packing it with gauze and taping it with more fresh bandages. She went into one of the bedrooms and got pillows and comforters in order to make the woman as comfortable as she possibly could. She then made herself some tea, got pillows and a comforter for herself, and went to sleep on the bathroom floor.

***

Danesha exited her home in Carmel. Locking the door, she scoped the block from the left to right. Counting the cars in the neighborhood, she hit the button on her keychain disarming the car alarm. Eyeing the house with a for rent sign across the street from where she lived she stared for a few seconds. She made a mental note to check it out later tonight. One could never be too careful. She knew that law enforcement agencies used homes like that to set up surveillance. Reaching for the driver's door she paused, turned, and looked down the block once more. She spotted a dark blue Sedan parked a little ways down on the opposite side of the street that just screamed cop. She found herself staring eye to eye with Detective Jackson as he smiled and waved while slowly pulling up next to her.

Double parking he left the engine running and climbed out. "Andrews."

"Jackson. I didn't know you were a part of the neighborhood watch. I didn't see you at any of the meetings."

"I was actually waiting for you."

She held her hands out. "I'm here."

"You know another one of your girls bit the dust last night?"

Danesha wasn't surprised. "No, I didn't. We aren't girls as you so put it. We haven't spoken for almost twenty years. Am I the number one suspect in this one too?"

"You're definitely on the list." He eyed her suspiciously. "You aren't going to ask who it was?"

She opened her car door and climbed in. "You want to question me speak—"

Jackson threw up his hand and nodded. "To your union rep. Yeah, I know. I got 'em on speed dial."

Danesha started the car and shifted into drive before pressing the down button on her window. "Tell me this, Jackson... How can you afford a car like that again? That's a million dollar machine." She looked over at his ride.

"You tell me. You're a detective."

Danesha hit the gas and the car leaped from the curb. She swerved almost hitting Detective Jackson. Watching through her rearview mirror she laughed as she bent the corner. Aiello wanted to meet. About what she wasn't sure. If she had to guess, it would be to sweat her about a buyer for the product. Aiello could be such a pest at times. Pulling up to the light, she checked behind her making sure that Jackson wasn't tailing her. Reaching into her ashtray, she grabbed a bag of coke, sprinkled a little on the back of her hand, and snorted a line. The light changed and she continued on. It wasn't long before she was pulling into the lot at Manny's warehouse. She crept in slowly as she watched Manny exit the building followed by a man she'd never met. She pulled up behind Aiello's black on black Chevy SS and parked. He stood next to his car watching her approach. Climbing out of her ride she nodded at the men.

Manny approached and shook her hand. "How are you?"

"I'm all right, Manny." She shot a cautious look towards the newcomer. "What's this all about?"

Osama extended his hand to her. "I'm Osama and you are?"

Aiello intervened smacking his hand away from Danesha's reach. "What the hell you care who we are? You need a name? I'm guy and she's girl."

Osama's face scrunched in anger.

Aiello ignored him focusing his attention on Manny. "What's the deal, Manny? And what's Bin Laden got to do with it?"

Osama balled his fists and moved towards Aiello. Aiello didn't budge but before Osama could reach him, Manny pushed Osama back.

"Wait over there," Manny advised him. "Let us talk."

"Screw this." Osama kicked his foot in the loose gravel and dust blew into Manny and Aiello's faces. He turned and walked away.

"Sorry about that." Manny looked at his brother-in-law apologetically.

"You know better than that, Manny."

"I said sorry." Manny's voice escalated just a little. "Look, I found a way to move the product. Osama has—"

Danesha intervened having heard something that finally struck her attention following the show of male ego. "Product? What is he talking about, Aiello?"

"I needed a place to sit on it. That's what you said, right? So I'm sitting on it. Over at my sister's place."

Danesha frowned. "Jesus, I can't believe you two! Now we bringing in third world representatives into the deal? Are y'all fuckin' stupid?"

Manny rolled his eyes. "What are you talking? Third world? He's from Detroit."

"I wouldn't give a damn if he was from your mother's snatch. I don't know him and I don't trust him."

"I checked him out. He's the real deal."

Danesha laughed. "You did, did you? Not only are you a big time dealer now you freelance as a detective on the side too right?"

"I ran a check." Manny was offended.

"Oh great! You hear that, Aiello?" She smiled at her partner sarcastically. "A background check. What did this check tell you?"

"He did ten years for distribution."

She didn't respond verbally. She shook her head disbelievingly.

Aiello placed his hand on Manny's chest. "Give us a few minutes alright."

Manny threw his hands in the air and walked off towards Osama.

Aiello ran his hand through his hair. He needed to diffuse this situation. "I know it was dumb and reckless."

"You think so?"

"Let me talk to the guy, get a feel for him. I'll check him out. The right way... and I'll let you know."

Danesha wasn't feeling it. "Are you serious? There are too many factors that can go wrong even if he does check out. Do me a favor and tell this guy to forget about us. Let me worry about selling the product and for Christ's sake get your brother-in-law under control."

Before he could respond, she got into her car and backed out of the parking lot. Aiello pounded his fist into his palm. He contemplated the situation as Manny and Osama waited and watched. Taking a breath, he approached the men stopping eye to eye with Osama. "Manny told you what we had?"

"What... but not how much or the quality."

"A hundred twenty pounds give or take a few pounds."

"Give me a day or two. Do I go through Manny or you want me to—"

"Who is your guy?"

"My cousin."

"Sorry, that doesn't do it for me."

"Oh okay. Well, they call him fuck off, none of your business. I don't get your name you don't get his."

"What we have here is what they call a Mexican standoff, my friend. No offense, Manny."

Manny grunted.

Osama stood his ground. "I can't do it any other way."

"Fuck off." Aiello turned to walk away.

Osama did the same turning to go back into the warehouse.

Manny threw his hands in the air in frustration. "Wait! Wait! The two of you hold on. There has to be room for compromise somewhere, right?"

Both men paused.

Osama turned and faced Aiello. "I'm willing to try if he is."

Aiello's back was still to the two men. "We've already met right?"

"Right..."

"Let's keep it like that. You act as a middle man and I never have to meet fuck off and he never has to meet me. I'll throw in a little extra from my cut for your middleman fee."

"He should go for it. I'll see what he says."

"Talk to him. Bring what he says back to Manny."

***

They had been hiding out for the past few days and the woman was slowly getting her strength back. Niome was proving useful. As the woman took inventory of her arsenal and ammunition, she watched as Niome cleaned the gun just as she had taught her. She'd gotten rid of the postal truck and brought back the things she needed to remove the bullet from her side. They only spoke to one another when necessary. She still had no idea who Niome was and who her mother was. She charged it to the game thinking it was only fair since the girl had no idea who she was either and she had no intentions of telling her. It was no doubt in her mind that they would get Carlene but how it ended between the two of them was still in the air.

"You know, you never told me your name," Niome stated disrupting their silence. "You know my name. I think it's a fair exchange."

"It's your night to cook, kid." The woman ignored Niome's inquiry.

"Yeah, I know." Niome was disappointed. "I'll get to it as soon as I clean these last two guns."

She can see that the girl was a dedicated worker. "Leave 'em. I'll get to it."

Niome didn't argue. She finished the gun she was working on and made her way to the kitchen.

A while later the woman entered the kitchen, poured them both a glass of wine, and sat Niome's glass on the counter. "Cheyenne," she said bluntly pushing the glass towards Niome.

Niome looked at her blankly for a moment then caught her meaning. Choosing not to make a big deal out of her finally sharing her name she looked away and continued working. "I don't drink." She grilled the onions to top the turkey burgers she was frying.

"You do tonight. A glass or two will help you relax and sleep better. We're doing the job tomorrow."

Niome set the two plates of food on the counter and joined her. She bowed her head in prayer. Cheyenne drank her wine as she watched the young girl silently pray over the food.

"You're a pretty good cook, kid." Cheyenne took a hearty bite out of her burger.

"Had to learn. It was only me and mama all my life. Never knew my father or any other family. When I was a kid, I stopped asking about my dad 'cause mama beat that out of me. I suppose she was doing the best she knew."

The room became awkwardly quiet. The two ate and drank. Twenty minutes later Niome broke the silence. "Do you have any children?"

Cheyenne bit her lip. The veins protruded from her neck. She stuffed a handful of fries in her mouth. While still chewing she took a huge gulp of wine and poured another glass.

Sensing her partner's discomfort Niome avoided eye contact and ran her finger around the rim of her wine glass. "Forget about it. You don't have to answer that."

Cheyenne cleared her throat. "You're a nice looking kid. How come you don't have a boyfriend?"

"Why is it that you can ask me personal questions, but I can't ask you?"

"This is my house. That's why."

"This is your house and you can ask." Niome shrugged her shoulders, picked up her plate and glass, and placed them in the sink. "But I don't have to answer. I'm going to bed."

"It's not too late, kid. I wouldn't think any less of you if you skipped out tomorrow."

"As much as I appreciate that," Niome replied sarcastically. "The truth is I don't give a damn what you think of me. We have a job to do tomorrow and I'm going to see it through."

"You know that comes with a price don't you?"

"We all gotta pay in one way or another."

"Night, kid."

Niome didn't respond. She walked to her bedroom and closed the door.

***

Nicolai felt like crap. He had no one to turn to and was fresh out of options for ways to find and get Eli's product back without admitting to being an informant. He had been calling and paging Aiello and Danesha for the past two days and neither were answering or returning his calls. He sat in his car outside of the two-bedroom house he was renting in Indianapolis. His wife had left and took their daughter with her to Israel. Eli had his home burned to the ground and threatened to have his people in New Jersey hunt his mother down and have her head delivered in a jar if he didn't get his product back. He'd told Eli everything he could about the detectives without telling on himself. He had no one to help him. His worthless cousin was living with him in the house he was renting but he had no connections.

Nicolai was drunk and afraid. Taking a swallow of the Jack Daniels he had in his lap he threw the open bottle on the back seat and pulled out his revolver placing it in his mouth. He could taste the dirty metal on his tongue. The scent of gun powder invaded his nostrils. He pulled back the hammer, closed his eye, and his cell phone rang. His heart rate quickened as he slowly released the hammer and dropped the gun on the floor by his feet. Crying he reached for his phone and pressed the talk button.

"Where you at, Cuz?"

Nicolai remained silent.

"Hello, you there?"

"Yeah, I'm here. I'm outside. Unlock the door. I'm coming in." Nicolai ended the call. He got out of the car, walked the few feet from the car to the house, and walked in. "What is it?" he asked as he flopped down on the used furniture he'd picked up from the thrift store.

"What's wrong with you?" Osama asked as he handed Nicolai a beer.

"Nothing."

"No worries, cousin. I have a plan to make all over your troubles go away."

Nicolai wanted no part of whatever his cousin had cooked up. He was bad news and he'd had enough bad luck in his life. "No, thank you. Why didn't you just go back to Israel with Basheera?"

Osama was his cousin by marriage so he was really Basheera's cousin. Osama answered with a shrug of the shoulders. "What is there for me? In America, a man with a plan can become millionaire."

"A plan huh?"

"Yes. American dream is ours, right?"

Nicolai popped the cap off of his Miller High Life and the suds from the beer drizzled down the side of the bottle. He ignored the mess and guzzled the cold beer as it dripped over his hands onto the floor. "Forget about it, Osama. Whatever you have in mind is nowhere near enough for what I need to get Eli off my back."

"Trust me. I think this might be it. At least come and see what he has."

"I pass."

"As a favor... It's a quick two man job... In and out. You can maybe use your cut to buy some more time with Eli."

"I don't owe you any favors."

"Do this and I'll owe you one. What do you have to lose?"

"You want to be Jessie James. Just go right in and bang, bang rob this man right?"

Osama laughed. "No. No bang, bang. This guy won't be a problem. You should really think about doing this."

Nicolai took one final swig from his bottle finishing it off. Osama, who had yet to even open his, handed his bottle to Nicolai. Nicolai took the bottle and rubbed the cold glass across his forehead to cool his flesh. He closed his eyes. "I'll think about it."

***

Today was the third day of her lessons. She had learned some quick self-defense moves, how to shoplift, and steal cars. She'd also picked up on a few cons that might get her out of a tight situation if need be. She knew it would be difficult because Cheyenne hadn't talked about it. She usually prepared her for the lesson the day before by letting her know what they were going to be doing and why it was important. Today was different. Today they were at the downtown library.

"You know how to use the internet, kid?"

"Sure I do. What's up?"

"Look up known sex offenders living in Indianapolis."

Niome sat down in front of the computer, logged on, and keyed in sexual offenders in Indianapolis through a search engine. The Public Record Repository popped up at the top of the list. She clicked on the link and the website opened up. Rows and rows of men convicted of sexual assault of one crime or another appeared on the screen.

Niome's nose scrunched up as if she caught wind of a foul stench. "Now what?" She asked confusedly.

"Pick one."

"Pick one for what?"

"To die."

"You're kidding right?"

"What was our agreement?"

"Do what you say, no questions." She inhaled then exhaled. "Ian Bell."

"Let me see." Cheyenne leaned in closer to the screen. "Ian Bell, 5'9, 145 pounds. Convicted of rape, sexual battery, and possession of child

pornography, sexual misconduct with a minor, and lewd assault. This
guy is a real sweetheart here."

Niome turned her head from the screen.

Cheyenne stood. "Let's go hunting."

***

Detective Jackson sat at his desk going over all the notes he had taken
and sifted through homicide photos. The chief was on his back to
get results about the Love case. He told him he was making progress,
but that was all a lie. He had pieces of the puzzle only he had no
idea how they all fit. The first murder started the mystery: the former
Governor Love. He picked up her book and sifted through the pages.
He'd bought a copy and read it. Nothing in the book foretold of this
coming. He set the book down and looked at crime scene photos
of Nicole Gleman. There was no murder weapon and no sign of her
supposed daughter. That was another thing. Who was this mysterious
woman?

Detective Jackson had questioned the caretaker at the building.
He'd known nothing about the two women; only that they claimed
to be mother and daughter. He wanted to press charges whenever she
was found for knocking out his teeth. From the way, he described the
item used to alter his appearance it sounded like the murder weapon.
His assailant, this Niome Gleman, was otherwise a ghost. No one had
seen or ever heard of her. She didn't even have a birth certificate on
file. The only lead he had was that the old man was paid to let Carlene
Stone know if any strangers came lurking around which the old man
says never happened.

Detective Jackson stood and stretched. Sitting back down, he
propped his feet up on his desk. There has got to be a connection, he
thought. He set his feet back on the floor and thumbed through his
notepad. He had questioned the warden and a few guards who dealt
with Cheyenne Cox at the prison on a day to day basis. None had

anything applicable to say about her in one way or another which he found odd. All of their stories were similar and somewhat rehearsed. He questioned a few inmates also. They all had the same stories as the guards and warden. Someone was definitely hiding something.

Before he'd left one woman whispered to check Cheyenne's medical files. In exchange, he promised to keep her name out of it. If anything came of it, he would owe her one when she was released from prison. He still hadn't checked the medical records. He had them sitting on his desk. He was also waiting to get the results back from the medical examiner about the blood that was found on Nicole's hand. He tried to bring Carlene Stone in for questioning, which was a no go. She'd said if she weren't under arrest he could fuck off. "Yeah," he said to himself. "These broads are hiding something."

Detective Lumpkins stopped by his desk and dropped a file in his lap. Detective Jackson opened it up and looked at it. It was crime scene photos of a dead postal worker. He didn't get it. "What's this?"

"A case I caught a few days ago."

"Yeah?"

"Thought it might have a connection with your Love case."

"Why is that?" Detective Jackson quickly read through the notes. "Neither of my cases involved strangulation. It says here that your guy was choked to death."

"He was jacked for the postal truck. Today someone reported that a postal truck was sitting out in front of their house for a few days. They never saw anyone come or go. A black and white checks it out and come to find out it's our missing truck."

"Uh- huh?" Jackson was waiting for the point where he should give a fuck.

"We ran the truck for prints and found this." Lumpkins held up a plastic evidence bag containing a jagged knife. He handed it to Detective Jackson. "I remember hearing you say you were looking for a big serrated knife. Thought this might be it."

"Please tell me you got prints." The coincidence was a stretch and Jackson needed something solid to make it relevant.

Lumpkins shook his head. "Sorry."

"Damn. What about off the truck?"

"Wiped it clean."

"Come on, Lumpkins." This entire conversation was going nowhere quickly.

"All but the keys in the ignition." Lumpkins smiled.

Detective Jackson stood to his feet. "You got a print?"

"A partial off the ignition key. They were thorough, just not thorough enough. Also looks like there may be remnants of blood that they missed when wiping down the handle of the knife. I'm thinking it's probably the victim's, but you never know."

"Are they in the system?"

"No hits. Just thought I would keep you in the loop."

"Thanks, man. I'd like to run that knife down to the medical examiner if that's alright?"

"Cool with me. Let me know anything comes of it."

"Will do."

Detective Lumpkins walked off as Detective Jackson picked up a copy of Cheyenne's medical history he obtained from the prison hospital and began reading it.

***

It was the third time that Nicolai had checked the clip in his gun. He couldn't believe he allowed Osama to talk him into going along with this stupid scheme to rob this man. He sat in the passenger seat as Osama drove finding himself becoming more annoyed with each passing minute. No matter what Osama did it got under his skin. He drove too slow and Nicolai complained. He drove too fast and he still complained. He had the radio off so Nicolai complained that it was too quiet. Osama slid a CD in and Nicolai's expression turned into a scowl at the sound of the rap music that accosted his ears. Nicolai didn't say anything thinking it was useless. He felt like the entire situation was a bad cliché: riding in a crappy car with guns listening to 2 Chains on their way to go rob a man. If the situation wasn't so sad, it might have been funny.

Nicolai laughed to himself as he rolled down the window. "Does this man own a firearm?"

"Manny? No. I mean... I don't think so."

"You don't think so?"

"No. Definitely not."

Nicolai shook his head. "When we get there I'll carry in the duffle bag with the telephone books."

"Okay. Why are we bringing the bag full of telephone books again?"

Aggravated Nicolai tapped his forehead softly with the barrel of his gun. "Think, Osama. It is a prop. I doubt this man has ever seen a million dollars in cash. We'll use it as a prop. Walk in, you introduce me, I drop the bag by my feet telling him it is cash, you flash the real money which I gave you." Nicolai looked at him suspiciously. "You still have the fifty thousand I gave you?"

Osama shook his head yes as he reached underneath his seat and removed the brown paper bag. "Right here."

"Good. If he is like most men, which I'm willing to bet he is, greed will win out over common sense. He will forget about his partner and rush to get the drugs with a million dollars at his feet."

"I understand. But why go through with all of this if we are just going to take it anyway?"

"You never heard the saying you get more bees with honey than vinegar? Let him give us what we want willingly. Once we see what he has is legit then we flash the guns and take it all."

Osama nodded in agreement smiling. "You sure you've never done this before?"

"Never mind that. Just pay attention when we get there. Stay alert."

"I am. Just relax. Everything is going to go fine."

Nicolai tucked his gun into his holster as they pulled up in front of the house. He looked up and down the block. It seemed no different than any other suburban neighborhood. "You ready?"

Osama grabbed the brown bag and got out of the car. He closed the door and tucked the bag under his arm. "Let's go."

Nicolai opened his door and got out walking around to the trunk. Osama popped the trunk with the press of a button on his key chain. Nicolai reached in and pulled out a duffel bag. "Which house is it?" Nicolai looked from house to house.

"Right here," Osama said as he tilted his head at the house they were standing in front of. "He said come through the garage...that the side door would be open."

The two men walked up the driveway to the garage door and walked in. Manny was sitting in a chair listening to sports on the radio. He stood to his feet and approached the two men with his hand out. He shook both of their hands as Osama introduced him to Nicolai. Manny wanted to question Osama about Nicolai. It was clear that the two were not related, but he kept it to himself. He just wanted to get the introduction out of the way and set a price and date for the deal to go down. He was starting to regret allowing Osama to talk him into doing it so soon. Aiello hadn't even gotten back to him yet about the check he was doing on Osama.

Manny cleared his throat. "What you have in the bag?"

Nicolai remained silent. Manny felt a sense of uncomfortableness fall over him. Osama stepped forward. Smiling, he placed the brown paper bag into Manny's hand. Manny opened the bag and his eyes became wide staring at the stacks of hundred dollar bills rolled into rubber bands.

"Fifty thousand," Osama stated. "The rest is in that bag. It's yours depending on how much product you have. We showed you the fifty thousand as a show of good faith. Now it's time for you to show us the same courtesy. Let us see the stuff."

Manny hesitated. Something didn't seem right to him yet he went to the truck anyway and removed one of the duffel bags. He dropped it on the floor near Osama's feet. "This isn't all of it. The rest is in another location. This is just a show of faith, as you put it, to discuss price." Manny hoped they believed his lie as he watched Osama kneel down and unzip the bag.

Stacked neatly in the duffel bag sat rolls of brown bricks of Heroin sealed with duct tape all stamped with a black widow spider on the top. Osama picked up a kilo and handed it to Nicolai. "Does it look good, 'Cuz?"

Nicolai's breath was literally taken away as he stared at the symbol of the black widow. Maybe his problems were answered. He felt a sense of excitement rush through him as a smile took root across his face. He knew that symbol. He had seen it before. It was the same symbol he'd seen plastered across the crates on the back of a U-Haul truck Kendricks took him to at the storage unit. This was Eli's dope. Nicolai looked down at the bag full of drugs then at Osama and Manny. He laughed.

***

Cheyenne and Niome sat outside Ian Bell's house on 24th and Franklin waiting for him to come home. Niome told her it wasn't necessary and that she didn't need the practice. She tried to convince her that when it was time to do Carlene she would just do it and she wouldn't freeze up or hesitate. Cheyenne wouldn't hear of it. She wanted it done up close and personal. Niome was nervous. She flicked the switchblade Cheyenne had given her open and close, open and close.

"Would you cool it with the knife, kid?"

Niome closed the knife and slipped it into an all black hoodie she was wearing. Her long black hair was pulled back into a ponytail tucked underneath a black skull cap. "What is taking him so long to get home?"

"Relax, kid. You got some place to be?"

"It's nerve wrecking waiting so long. We've been here almost four hours. He needs to get here so we can get this over with already."

"A major part of the kill is waiting. Always waiting for something."

"Patience ain't never been an attribute of mine."

"You'll learn."

"Is that him?"

"You don't remember?"

"You wouldn't let me print out his picture."

"What's one of the rules?"

"No physical evidence linking me to the crime if I can help it."

"That's right. That means no photos of the targets, no slips of papers with numbers or addresses, no cell phones that you can't toss...only prepaid phones if you got to have a phone... No emails. Do I need to go on?"

"No, I got it. Memorized everything. I got it. It's him."

"You remember what to do?"

"I do."

"Then do it."

Niome opened the door and got out of the car. Closing the door, she made quick steps to catch up with her prey. Hands in her pockets head held low she felt her palms getting sweaty. Her breathing got light. "Yo!" She screamed out at his back.

He stopped and turned to face her. Walking closer, she was now eye to eye with Ian Bell. She knew what she had to do and if anyone deserved it, it was him.

"Yeah? Do I know you, cutie?" Ian asked with a foul smile, breath smelling like dog crap, and his bottom row of teeth missing.

Niome stood frozen staring up at the man whose life she was supposed to end.

"I know you ain't mute, honey. I just heard your voice."

"I... I... I." She stuttered taking a step and removing the knife. She flicked the blade out nervously. He immediately grabbed her wrist backing her up against a wall. She struggled and fought to not let him get the knife. Just as she kneed him in the balls, she heard the sound of flesh ripping and a girlish like squeal escape his lips.

He fell forward with his eyes wide. Stepping to the side, she watched him hit the ground. Cheyenne stood behind him. She knelt down shoving the knife deeper into his back then yanking it out effortlessly. Without a word, she walked back to the car.

Niome quickly followed behind. "You didn't have to do that. I had it under control."

"You froze up, kid. You didn't do what I told you to do."

"I couldn't. I..."

"He was a piece of crap. The world is better off. Maybe knives aren't your thing."

"Maybe not."

"You better find out what it is real soon."

Niome handed her the knife back and climbed into the passenger seat.

**

Aiello lay in bed thinking about his life and the decisions he'd made along the way. Slaving at a dead end job for piss pay was what he'd been doing for years. That would all be over in a day or two and he would be a millionaire. He couldn't quit the force right away, but he was seriously considering taking a desk job. His phone rang interrupting his daydream. Looking at the Caller Id, he saw that it was Manny. He pressed the talk button and spoke into the phone. "What's going on Manny?"

"Nothing much. I meant to call you earlier today. Your sister has been bugging me about getting you over for dinner."

"Oh, shit. I thought you were going to say that she said something about the truck."

Manny laughed. "No. She fussed a little bit in the beginning, but she's cool now. As long as everything works out when it's supposed to and we get it out of here fast she should leave the situation alone."

"Cool."

There was an awkward pause. Manny cleared his throat before speaking. "Say how about stopping and getting a bottle of wine before you come over."

Aiello sighed. He didn't really feel up to going out, but he unenthusiastically agreed. "Alright. Give me thirty minutes."

Manny half-heartedly laughed. "See you when you get here."

Aiello ended the call, climbed out of bed, and tripped over his cowboy boots hitting his knee on the television stand. He felt the pain shoot through his leg giving him an instant headache. Picking up his jeans from the floor, he slid them on and hurriedly pulled on his boots. He snatched up his shirt, gun, and badge and dashed out the door. Stopping by the liquor store, he grabbed a bottle of red wine and a pack of cigarettes. Before long he was parked in front of Manny's garage. Getting out of the truck, he reached for his cell to call Manny. Instantly the garage door opened. The first thing he noticed was that his truck was gone. The second thing he noticed was his brother-in-law sitting in a chair surrounded by three men all holding submachine guns. Manny's eyes diverted to the floor.

"Manos arriba!" One of the men screamed out to him while waving his gun in Aiello's direction.

Aiello paused. He didn't have to know Spanish to know to put his hands up and not make any sudden moves. He put his hands in the air still clutching the wine bottle in his left hand. "What's going on here?" Aiello demanded as he took a step towards the three men.

"No mueva gringo!"

Aiello gritted his teeth. The door to the kitchen opened and Osama stood in the doorway with a look of triumph on his face and a smile on his lips. He nodded his head towards the other side of the door. "Inside," he demanded.

Aiello hesitated. His thoughts raced. The more he thought about it the dumber he felt. He didn't know what he was walking into or against once he stepped inside that house. Backup would be good right about now, he thought. There was no one he could trust other than Danesha and he knew he'd burnt that bridge with her when he'd gone through with the deal after she told him not to. No turning back, he thought to himself as he stepped forward towards the door.

Manny whimpered as Aiello passed him. "I'm sorry. I didn't mean to set you up. I had no choice."

"Silencio!" The man standing behind Manny smacked him across the back of the head with his gun.

Manny dropped his face to his knees as he gripped the back of his head. He felt blood seeping through his fingers as his head began to throb. Aiello shook his head distressingly. Manny could be so stupid at times. Aiello questioned himself now. He didn't know who the bigger fool was: him for not listening to Danesha or his brother-in-law for trying to make the deal happen without him.

Osama stepped to the side as Aiello entered the kitchen. Before he was in the house good, he felt a strong blow to his lower abdomen followed by a punch to the back of the head. Falling forward, he dropped the wine bottle and caught himself on the kitchen counter in the center of the kitchen. Pushing himself back to his feet, he turned grabbing Osama by his shirt. He pulled him close kneeing him in the groin when he doubled over in pain. Aiello pulled his gun and had it pointed in Osama's face. Osama began to <u>cower</u> with his hands up. Aiello paused as he heard weapons cocking back in the room. He assumed they were all pointed at him.

"Drop it, Aiello!"

Aiello recognized the voice. He dropped his weapon and slowly turned around with his hands in the air. For the first time upon entering the house, he was able to adequately survey his surroundings. Positioned to the left of him stood two men both with guns trained on him. Nicolai stood directly in front of him with a gun aimed at his mid-section. Aiello didn't know who was more frightened, Nicolai or his brother-in-law in the garage. Focusing his attention on the scene in the living room he spotted his sister, Marie, staring at him tears sitting in the wells of her eyes. Her two daughters sat at her feet. The house was eerily quiet. Across from Marie Aiello saw a man sitting in the chair opposite of her. He had his back to the kitchen so all Aiello saw was the top of his head. Aiello tilted his head looking at Osama from the corner of his eye and turned up his lip in contempt. "Your cousin my ass."

Osama held his stomach. He felt a sharp pain from being hit in the groins. He struggled to speak. "He is my cousin through marriage."

"Let the woman and children go. You have the product. Keep this between us."

Nicolai slowly raised the gun at Aiello so that it was eye level. Aiello felt his body temperature rise as he contemplated reaching out and taking the gun from Nicolai. He thought better of it figuring they might let his sister and nieces go if he cooperated. Nicolai waved the gun in the direction of the living room. Aiello sullenly moved in that direction with Nicolai following close behind him with a gun pressed into his back.

Aiello stopped a few inches short of his sister. "You alright?"

She nodded yes as she wiped the tears from her eyes. The girls sniffled trying their best not to cry too loudly. He looked down into their faces and felt pain pierce his heart as they stared back up at him with fear etched across their tiny faces. That feeling of sorrow quickly diminished and resurrected itself as anger. "Don't worry, ladies. This will be over soon. I'll take care of everything."

"Will you now?" The mystery man sitting across from Marie was intrigued.

"Who the hell are you?" Aiello asked venomously now ignoring Nicolai.

"I am Eli Li Calzi. Have a seat Detective Valentino Aiello. We have much to discuss."

"I'm not discussing a damn thing until you let my sister and her children go."

Nicolai stepped forward with his gun aimed at Aiello's face. A look of eagerness blanketed his face, but relief and desperation shone in his eyes. He knew down in his heart he was no killer but he would do the deed if it meant keeping Aiello quiet about his cooperating with him and his partner. Eli raised his arm brushing Nicolai's action off. Nicolai didn't try to mask his disappointment as he lowered the weapon stepping back angrily and grunting in disapproval.

Eli pointed towards the sofa across from where he sat. "I'm asking you nicely sit. We talk. I promise only talking for now. If it goes another way, it will be you that makes it, go that way."

Aiello huffed and sat. "You want to talk, I'm listening."

"I have two questions and you will answer both of them honestly."

Aiello didn't respond. He stared back at Eli with his eyebrow raised as a smirk creased his lower lip.

Eli was unfazed. "I want to know how to find your partner and my product."

"That's one question."

"The second one is critical. Almost as important as the first."

"I'm listening."

"One, all I need is one, reason not to kill you and all your family."

"I don't need threats as motivation to compromise or cooperate. It's counterproductive and all it does is anger me."

Eli didn't respond.

Aiello's eyes narrowed. "First, this is not how I discuss business. Not in a room full of people and definitely not in front of women and children. Come on, Eli. Let's be men about the situation and conduct business as men do."

Eli leaned back in his seat and crossed his leg one over the other. "Detective, do you know how to get the truth out of a man?"

Aiello leaned forward with his hands on his knees. "I usually bring them as near to the edge of death as possible without pushing them over."

Eli smirked knowingly at Nicolai. Nicolai swallowed trying desperately to mask his discomfort with a phony tough guy expression. His forehead wrinkled and the fire in his eye was barely a flicker as the only people he fooled in the room were Marie and her daughters.

Eli sighed. "Nicolai, you and the others take the woman and the girls to the garage with the husband. Go! Let the men talk."

Nicolai's face turned as pale as bleached flour. Had he thought he could make it out alive he would have killed them both right there. He knew he was on borrowed time. All he could do was pray that Aiello didn't use him as a bargaining chip to save his own life. Nicolai hesitated before tucking his gun in the holster and motioning with his hand for the ladies to move towards the garage.

Once the house was cleared Eli scooted his chair closer to Aiello so that they were face to face. "Make it good, young man." Eli crossed his legs once more folding his hands and placing them on top of his knee.

Aiello leaned in closer speaking in a whispered tone and looking over his shoulder as if he expected to be overheard or interrupted at any moment. "I will get your product back. Not for my life or to save my family... I do this as a show of good faith."

"Okay, I'll bite. Good faith for what?"

"I'm going to go to work for you. And before you say anything, Mr. Li Calzi, you can't say your organization doesn't need the help. That jerk off Nicolai is just the tip of the iceberg, of no fault of your own, in a long line of screw ups."

"You're going to work for me?" Eli asked pointing to himself with his thumb.

"Yes, sir. Let's say you pay me fifty large a month."

Eli considered it. "One thing at a time. Where are Detective Andrews and my product?"

"I promise you I will get it back, clean up your house, and send a clean and clear message that the Li Calzi family runs Indiana. I will eradicate any other family doing business in the state be it Russians, Jamaicans or any Outlaw motorcycle gang. I will give you tips on raids going down, keep the heat off your guys, and any large shipments we take down I will sell a quarter of it to you at a discount."

"Interesting. You know how they say...uh... Beware of strangers that bear gifts."

Aiello shrugged his shoulders.

Eli was intrigued. "What is this you say of screw ups in my organization?"

"You have a snake amongst you."

Eli didn't like that this cop knew more about the weak links within his crew than he did himself. "Who?"

"Do I have the job?" Aiello needed some kind of guarantee that he was in the clear.

"I will not bargain with you. You will tell me now!"

"Or what?"

"We will see how long it takes to push your sister to the edge of death. We will see if you break before I push her over."

"The way I see it, if we don't make a deal right here and now we're all dead anyway. Do what you have to do. I'm sure you'll even make it again but the other two million dollars' worth of product is still out there and I can get it back. You will find out about the snake amongst you as well. The only question is will you find out before it's too late?"

"How do I know this is legit information? You won't even give me a name. Am I to just take your word?"

"We have to start somewhere."

Eli knew that this was more than likely a trick to buy the man time to try and warn his partner. But on the other hand he figured it was better to be safe than sorry. "That all sounds well and fine. We'll talk more about a permanent position after I get my product back. This Detective Andrews, how can I say....someone must be made an example of?"

Aiello stood to his feet and paced the room with his back to Eli. "She's like family. She's my partner."

"No. She is a co-worker. Your family is in the garage and it is your family whom I will execute if you don't come through."

Aiello sighed. "That sounded very much like a threat."

"Detective, this is business. What's more important? Your sense of honor or your sense of financial security?"

Aiello turned to face Eli. "Funny...I was asking myself the same thing, Mr. Li Calzi."

***

Six rapid shots let loose from the small caliber handgun Niome clutched inside the shooting range on 28th and Madison Ave. She felt the vibrations move through her arm causing her body to convulse. Cheyenne stood back watching. Niome wasn't great, but she wasn't horrible either. She hit the paper target three of the six times she fired and two were fatal shots in the lower torso area. She needs more practice, Cheyenne thought as she stepped up next to Niome clutching her Sig P320. She took aim and fired six shots in succession. Five shots hit the target dead in the chest. The last blow was a head shot. Cheyenne popped the clip and placed both the clip and the unloaded gun back into the black metal case and closed it.

"We'll knock off for the day," Cheyenne said as she headed towards the exit.

Niome followed behind dropping her gun into her jacket pocket. They walked down the corridor, out into the lobby, through the exit, and to the street. Cheyenne watched Niome as she walked with her head held low and shoulders slumped. Niome avoided eye contact.

"It'll be alright," Cheyenne told her. "A few more times and you'll get the hang of it."

"Probably not."

"Having second thoughts?" Cheyenne stopped walking mid-stride and faced Niome.

Niome turned her face from Cheyenne. "No. I told you I had to do this. I just don't know if guns are my thing."

"I don't know if we'll get close enough to gut her."

"Gut her? With a knife?"

"Like a pig."

"Uh, no." Niome stepped around Cheyenne and continued walking until she reached the car. They had stolen an SUV earlier that morning.

Cheyenne walked around to the driver's side and climbed in. She closed the door and started the truck just as Niome got in and closed her door. "How you going do this, kid, if you scared of guns and knives?"

"I never said I was scared. They're just not my thing."

Cheyenne pulled out into traffic. "Not your thing?"

"No."

"Maybe killing's not your thing. You ever been in a fight?"

Niome shrugged. "A few scuffles. Never full all out bar brawls or nothing like that."

"You ever tasted blood, or better yet rode on a roller coaster?"

"Really? Tasted blood?"

"Yes really. If you've ever been in a real fight, you know that you win some, you lose some. You might get a black eye, get your hair pulled, or lip busted. The taste of your own blood running into your mouth isn't uncommon. The sensation you feel when you get a good grip on your opponent in the middle of a tussle... Heart pumping, blood boiling, and adrenaline rushing. Courage and fear conflicting... Run or stay and fight. All of those thoughts and feelings and emotions will stir up inside of you at the moment of truth when you hold your target's life literally in the palm of your hand."

Niome leaned her head back against the headrest and closed her eyes. "What do you do?"

"Think about why I'm doing this and know in my heart that I'm righteous in my actions then I put an end to their life."

...post some shit on Twitter.

~Danesha Andrews

At Indiana University, Health North Hospital during mid-day Danesha parked in the staff only parking spot. She turned the car off, got out, and let her eyes scan the parking lot. Looking for a buyer for the product, she and Aiello stole from the storage unit and trying to get Cheyenne before she managed to get her was beginning to work her nerves. Jackson wasn't making it any easier. She had to do it all knowing that he may be nearby watching. Walking to the back of her car, she popped the trunk and removed a gift bag that read 'Get well soon'. Four large balloons were tied to the bag. Slamming the trunk closed she turned and made her way to the hospital entrance. Pausing near the door, she felt eyes on her. From her peripheral, she spotted a plain clothes cop smoking a cigarette and definitely watching her. She could always tell who the cops were. She'd been doing it all her life. She didn't acknowledge him. She just kept walking into the building and paused at the entrance. Turning to see if he was behind she saw that he wasn't and promptly focused her attention on a security guard standing nearby.

"Officer I need your help," she said looking up at the officer almost on the brink of tears.

"Yes, ma'am. What's wrong?" he asked with genuine concern.

Danesha smiled inwardly. She still had it. Ever since she was younger she could always make herself cry on cue. "Don't look directly at him but over my shoulder is a guy in a beige suit with curly hair."

The security guard looked over her shoulder just as the officer walked in. He focused his attention back on her. "Yes, ma'am. Is he bothering you?"

"He's my ex and he won't stop following me. I filed a restraining order yet he still follows me. I think he has a gun."

"Don't worry, ma'am. You stay here." He pushed her behind him and nodded at the nurse behind the counter. He approached the man in a beige suit as Danesha quietly slipped away.

Walking swiftly as more security guards and a police officer rushed past her she pushed the up button on the elevator and waited for the doors to open. Once they did she stepped into the elevator. Riding to the fourth floor, she got off gift bag and balloons still in hand. She walked down the hall until she reached the room she was looking for. Two black guys wearing almost identical outfits. Leather black dress shoes, black slacks, one in a black turtle neck the other in a black sweater both covered in waist length black leather jackets, their heads shaven bald stood outside the door. As she approached the men, she knew that they were there as security. She attempted to walk in as if they were not standing there.

The shorter of the two men held his hand out keeping her back at arm's length. He was almost touching her chest. She smacked his hand away. The other guard placed his hand inside his jacket.

"I'm here to see Darryl," Danesha stated.

"Yeah? Who are you?"

"Fuck out of here! What do you mean who am I? Let me in." Once more she attempted to pass the two men by.

This time the first guy actually pushed her back. "No visitors."

Danesha grunted. "Look, I have this gift for him and I need to—"

"Leave it here with me. I'll make sure he gets it."

She hesitated. She didn't anticipate having to jump over hurdles to see him. "Here. It's a little gift bag I made up special for him. Can you respect our privacy and make sure only he sees it?"

The guard with his hand still on his gun inside his jacket smirked at Danesha letting his eyes roam seductively up and down her curvaceous frame.

The other guard sighed as he held out his hand to take the bag. "My word we won't look in the bag."

She handed the bag to the security guard, rolled her eyes, and then turned to walk off.

The guard with the bag watched her ass sway from side to side for a few seconds as she walked away then went into the room to take the gift bag into the man he was protecting.

"Yo, what's up with the bag?" He sat up.

The guard set the bag on a roll away tray in front of the bed. "I don't know. Some chick dropped it off and said it was personal between the two of y'all."

"Some chick? What she look like?"

The guard laughed. "She was bad."

"You ain't get a name?"

"Shit, how she was talking I figured it was probably naked pics or some shit in the bag. Thought you'd know who it was."

He leaned forward and grabbed the bag sitting it on his lap. "Man, these bitches crazy. Hoes know I got a wife and still coming here and shit. These bitches real bold."

The guard shook his head and turned to leave the room.

Darryl looked into the bag. "Hold up, G."

The guard paused and turned back to Darryl. "What's up?"

He reached into the bag and removed a brick of heroin. He instantly recognized the symbol of the black widow spider. He knew he had Eli's missing dope. "Fuck is this?"

The guard shrugged. "I didn't know. I told you I didn't look in the bag."

"Go get that broad, man!"

"Alright."

"Now, Nigga! Before the bitch leave the building."

The guard ran out of the room and returned quicker than Darryl had expected with Danesha in tow.

"You pat her down?" Darryl eyed her.

The guard spoke nervously. "She wouldn't let me boss."

"Wouldn't let you?"

"I have this thing about being touched." She flashed her badge.

"It'll never stick." Darryl crossed his arms.

"Hold on, let me tell you why I'm here before we get to calling lawyers and shit."

"I'm listening."

Danesha grabbed a chair and pulled it close to his bed. Staring up into his dark brown eyes was like staring into a black hole. It was dark and stirring yet she couldn't turn away. "We gon' make this a public meeting? You know call in the other guard, a few nurses, a doctor, post some shit on Twitter."

"Damn, shorty. You always this dramatic?"

He nodded at the guard. The guard nodded back and exited the room.

Danesha smiled and placed her hand on top of his nub where his hand used to be. "Thank you, Kendricks. I think we can do some business together."

***

Niome served as the driver chauffeuring Cheyenne around the city doing reconnaissance on Carlene Stone. Niome wanted her so bad she could taste it. Cheyenne taught her how to follow someone without being detected. It was exciting when she first began her lessons now after a week of doing nothing but driving and watching it was becoming a bit boring. They sat a block away watching Carlene and her entourage of cars outside Papa Roux's. That was her routine stop every Sunday after church. It made Niome think about her mom. Carlene had been bringing the two of them the sandwiches every Sunday for as long as she could remember.

"Are there other ways to kill?" Niome asked keeping her eyes focused on Carlene and her crew.

"Keep your eyes on the target."

"I am. I'm looking....are there?"

Cheyenne ignored the question.

"Cheyenne."

"What, kid? Damn!"

"I want to know."

"Just know this: the better you know your target's strengths, weaknesses, and habits the easier it is to get next to them and eliminate them."

"I see."

"You see? What the hell do you see?"

"Nothing."

Cheyenne looked over at Niome and grunted.

"Whatever, kid."

"Know the target's habits huh?"

"This is the deal. If I'm guessing right, she's going to be here around this time again next Sunday. We get here a half hour early and get in position around that area over there where they all parked at. They going to be comfortable because they're used to this environment. Boom there, there, and there." Cheyenne pointed to the three cars in

Carlene's convoy. "You let loose with the street sweeper. Just point and spray. The gun will do the rest. Whatever you don't hit I'll take care of with the chopper. I'm gon' drop Molotov's on the truck. You go in Papa Roux's and finish the driver. If Carlene, by the grace of God, makes it out of the truck alive I'll chop her up with the K."

Niome didn't respond.

"You listening to me, kid?"

Niome had her reservations about the plan working, but she kept them to herself. She nodded her head in agreement, put the car in drive, and pulled off.

***

Danesha barged through the door of the homicide precinct moving through the room in a quick, aggressive pace. Her eyes zeroed in on Detective Jackson as she made her way to him. Rudely she stepped in between him and the other cop he was talking to. Ignoring the other officer she pointed her finger in Jackson's face taking him by surprise.

"Back off, Jackson!" She issued a loud and stern warning. "It was funny at first but now it's just annoying."

Jackson looked over at the other officer. "Give me a minute, Lumpkins." He looked at Danesha then headed to his desk.

She followed him. "If you don't back off I'm going to file a grievance with I.A."

"We both know you're not going to do that. You're old school. I don't see you bitching and moaning to the upper brass let alone the rat squad. Besides, what has your panties in a bunch?"

"Don't play with me. I spotted your guy following me today."

"My guy? You're paranoid."

"This is the final warning, Jackson." She pushed his papers and laptop from his desk to the floor.

Everyone in the room focused their attention on the two of them.

His commanding officer stepped into the room. "Is there a problem, detectives?"

"No, sir," Jackson said as he watched Danesha walk towards the exit.

Out in the hall she pressed the down button on the elevator and waited. Lumpkins stood a few feet away talking to a group of beat cops. Danesha listened as he explained that they were going to serve an arrest warrant on a Courtney Awsum at his wife's funeral. They were going along as backup and Jackson was waiting for the warrant to get faxed over by a judge. Jackson wasn't backing down on this case. Going after Awsum, she thought. He was either ignorant or crazy. The elevator doors opened. She stepped inside and pressed the down button.

***

A week had gone since Aiello had held council with Eli and he still hadn't gotten the dope back or delivered Danesha to him. It wasn't from a lack of trying. He had been calling and leaving messages, but she never answered or returned his calls. They hadn't seen one another since the day they were introduced to Osama at Manny's warehouse. Their Captain told him she had requested some time off. She was definitely giving him the cold shoulder. The tail he put on her at the hospital failed miserably and she hadn't been back to her place in days. He knew he would only get one shot and to get her he would have to get creative. Leaving the meeting with Eli, he had to talk with Nicolai and his cousin. He didn't trust the two, but the way he saw it everyone had their use, even two screw ups like Nicolai and Osama.

They met at Washington Square mall. He walked into the Buffalo Wild Wings, took off his sunglasses, and spotted the two sitting at the bar drinking beer. He walked past the two and slid into a table with a booth. They followed suit joining him at the table. They both slid into the seat across from him.

The waitress walked up to the table immediately. "Can I start you gentlemen off with anything to drink?"

"No thank you," the three said in unison.

"I'll give you a few minutes." She walked off.

Aiello knew Nicolai was still on edge not knowing if he would spill the beans about him being an informant. Osama needed money now that he couldn't go back to work for Manny. He despised the fact that he now had to take orders from Aiello. He was sure that they would have their day and he tried his best not to sneer at Aiello as he spoke.

"Right here, right now it all starts new," Aiello advised.

The two men remained silent.

"Our only priority is getting Danesha and making sure she's never seen again." Aiello checked their faces for reaction.

Nicolai swallowed. "You're kidding right?"

"Do I look like I'm kidding? This is a business and this is how Mr. Li Calzi wants it. Someone has to be made an example of. Would you prefer it be you?" He paused for effect. "I can spin the story and make it go that way."

"What do you want us to do?"

"Find her and get rid of her. Literally. I don't want her body showing up."

"Why do we have to find her?" Osama's tone was laced with annoyance. "She's your partner."

"If it were that easy I wouldn't need you two dumbasses. If this is too much that means, you are useless to me and being useless is not a good position to be in right now."

Nicolai placed his hand on Osama's shoulder and shook his head. "Don't speak." He looked at Aiello. "We will take care of her."

Osama shrugged his shoulder removing Nicolai's hand and got up from the table. "I'll be out in the car." He stormed out of the restaurant just as Aiello's phone rang.

He looked at the Caller Id then pressed the talk button anxiously. "Where in the hell have you been?" He put his index finger to his lips indicating that Nicolai remain silent.

"Taking care of business. I see you've been calling." Danesha voice sounded annoyed on the other end of the phone.

"Yeah, only a few hundred times."

"Yeah sorry. I got some news for you that I thought you'll like. Let's meet."

"Give me twenty minutes and I'll meet you at your place."

"Naw. Meet me at the old warehouse where the insects were."

Aiello knew she was referring to the crates of Heroin with the stamps of the black widow. "Cool. Give me 'bout an hour though."

She ended the call without saying goodbye.

He set his phone on the table and grinned victoriously. "That was Danesha. She wants to meet. Here's what I want you to do." Aiello leaned across the table and whispered his instructions to Nicolai just as the waitress returned. Aiello stood to leave.

"Is there no other way? You ask for too much." Nicolai's voice was trembling.

"This is business, Nicolai. Nothing personal just business." He handed the waitress a ten dollar bill and shooed her away. Looking over at Nicolai, he spoke in a hushed tone. "Your secret is safe with me. Eli will never know. Just do this thing for me and the slate will be wiped clean between the two of us."

Apprehensive and squeamish Nicolai rose from the table and rushed out into the street almost knocking the waitress down as he left.

"Asshole!" she yelled out as she regained her bearings.

Aiello walked up to the waitress. "On second thought, sweetheart, make me some hot wings to go. I'll pay when I get back. I have to piss real quick." Aiello went to the bathroom and returned feeling good that things were beginning to turn in his favor. He paid the waitress and waited for his wings to get done. Sitting at the bar drinking beer he subconsciously patted his pockets looking for his phone. He stood to his feet and went back to the table that he'd been sitting at earlier. No phone. He looked underneath the table and still no phone. Going back to the bar, he asked the bartender and the waitress that took his order had anyone turned in a phone. They both told him no. Frustrated he took his wings and left.

***

Detective Jackson, followed by Detective Lumpkins and three additional squad cars, pulled up to the church on East 30th and park. With arrest warrant in hand Jackson got out of his car and proceeded to the entrance of the church as service was letting out. Awsum appeared from the sanctuary with his British assistant/bodyguard in tow. Jackson stepped to Awsum just as swarms of news vans pulled up to the scene. Reporters and cameramen rushed the church as Jackson placed the handcuffs on Awsum and ushered him into the back of his squad car.

"Trying to make this a high profile case, Jackson?" Lumpkins asked pointing to the media circus in front of them.

"High profile? Shit, it's already high profile. I'm investigating the murder of a former governor and arresting her husband. All the same, I didn't call these clowns."

"Well someone leaked it to 'em."

Jackson got into his car, slammed the door closed, and sped off.

Trust no man but God

~Nicolai

Nicolai drove in silence as Osama sat next to him and complained about Aiello and what he would do to him once this situation was all over. Nicolai was too pre-occupied to comment. He knew that this situation would never be over. It would be ongoing compounding problem after problem after problem until it consumed them all. Nicolai wanted to be the big man or at least that's the way he saw himself in his mind. But, the way the world treated him was different altogether. He was no more than an errand boy, a dupe, a lackey with a gun too afraid to take the world on and fight for what he wanted. Nicolai knew that blood would be shed. He knew that he would be the one to spill blood all in the name of keeping his secret. He thought of running but knew that would do no good. He had no money and men like Eli never went away. He would find him and kill him. That was for certain. Nicolai had no intentions of looking over his shoulder for the rest of his life.

"I don't trust him," Osama said breaking Nicolai from his thoughts. Nicolai laughed.

"What is funny?" Osama asked annoyed.

"It is funny to hear you speak of trust."

"I am funny now?"

"You say you do not trust him. You tell me how does one man gauge how much trust he should put in another man?"

"So when you have made your decision, put your trust in Allah. Certainly Allah loves those who put their trust in Him."

Nicolai laughed.

"There! Again you laugh." Osama was heated. "Do not mock God."

"I do not mock your God. I am laughing at myself."

Osama's eyebrow rose. "Yourself?"

"You have helped me in ways that you do not know. Thank you, cousin."

"Um, well... You are welcome. But how have I helped you?"

"I have a better understanding of trust and what must be done to move further in this situation with Aiello. I now see that I cannot trust you. There is no trust in man."

Osama was astonished. "That is not what I meant."

"I think it is. You made it clear. Trust no man but God." Nicolai raised his gun and shot Osama twice without hesitation. Once in the chest and once in the neck. Pulling over to the side of the road, he opened his car door and pushed him out. Slamming the door closed he put the car back in drive and pulled off. He fought back the vomit as he felt himself grow sick for what he had just done. Yeah, it will consume us all, he thought. I paid my debt to buy back my freedom from Aiello at my price... The death of my wife's cousin. Now I must pay back Eli. Nicolai pulled over to an abandoned lot, whipped the cell phone out, and made a call.

***

Courtney Awsum sat in the interrogation room. Detective Jackson sat across from him reading through papers in a manila folder. Neither man spoke the room was eerily silent. Detective Jackson smiled, closed the folder, and slid it across the table in front of Awsum. Awsum glanced down at the envelope. Placing his index finger down on the center of the folder he spun the folder in a circle. Both men watched as the folder slowly turned. As it stopped Awsum picked it up, opened it, and removed the paper. He carefully read the document. The form was not new to his eyes. He'd seen it before. It was a birth certificate. He placed it back into the folder, closed it, and slid it back to Detective Jackson.

"Why am I here, detective?" Awsum asked finally breaking the silence.

"You're here to help solve your wife's murder, Mr. Awsum."

"You had to handcuff me and embarrass me in front of my daughter on one of the most heart-wrenching days of my life?"

"Well, you know how we puppets are. Mr. Awsum."

Awsum smirked. "Following orders right?"

"Yes, sir."

"Very well. Get on with it."

"Are you?"

"Am I what?" Awsum asked hunching his shoulders.

"The father of Cheyenne's baby?"

"Where in the world did you come up with that? And what does it have to do with my wife's murder?"

"I have a theory."

"What's that?"

"A proposed explanation whose status is still conjectural and subject to experimentation in contrast to well-established propositions that are regarded as reporting matters of actual fact."

"And here I thought you were a Detective and you're nothing more than a second-rate comedian. I know what a theory is, Mr. Jackson. I'm asking you what yours is?"

Jackson smiled to mask the irritation he felt building inside. He didn't care for Awsum. He knew he was dirty and his smugness made it almost insurmountable to hold back his anger. Jackson stood and paced the room. "As you read in the folder there that is a copy of Cheyenne Cox's prison medical record."

"I don't see the connection."

"The proof is in the blood."

"Excuse me?"

"The blood, Mr. Awsum. As you and I both know, Cheyenne became pregnant a year after she was incarcerated."

"Don't be naïve, Detective. These things happen. So what?"

"So what? So what is, I'm going to need a DNA sample."

The door opened and the medical examiner entered carrying a metallic case. She closed the door behind her then set the case on the table and opened it. Removing a pair of plastic surgical gloves she slid them on then removed a long stemmed cotton swab. "Open up, Mr. Awsum."

"You must be out of your mind," he retorted as he leaned back in his seat folding his arms across his chest.

Jackson opened the manila folder and removed another form. He held it by two fingers dangling it in front of Awsum's face. "This here is a warrant signed by a judge allowing us to collect a saliva sample from you. We will get it even if we have to hold you down to get it."

The door once again swung open and a balding giant of a man stood in the doorway. "You will do no such thing!"

"Major Talbert!"

"Detective, this interrogation is over."

"The hell it is!" Jackson was livid.

"Excuse me? And I'd be very mindful of the next words coming out of your mouth, detective."

"Sir, I have a warrant for his DNA." Jackson pulled out the paper to support his claim. "The judge signed off on it. This is crucial to my investigation. I'm about to prove motive."

"Mr. Awsum, I apologize for the inconvenience. Sir, can you join me and the Mayor in the lieutenant's office."

Awsum stood to his feet buttoned his suit jacket. "Of course, Major. How are the wife and kids?"

"They are fabulous. I've been meaning to call you and thank you for the trip out to Maui. Can't get the kids to stop talking about it."

The two men, followed by the medical examiner, exited the interrogation room.

"Detective Jackson!" Major Talbert yelled out not stopping to look back.

"Yes, sir," Jackson responded stepping out of the interrogation room.

"You should join us in the lieutenant's office as well."

Jackson grudgingly followed behind as the two men made small talk and laughed. When Jackson stepped into his lieutenant's office, he saw that Awsum's bodyguard was already waiting. He was the last to enter the room. His heart settled when he realized that the Mayor wasn't actually in attendance. He stood in the doorway with the door still open and crossed his arms. "I guess the Mayor wasn't interested in participating in this ambush after all," he stated sarcastically.

"Better things to do," Major Talbert retorted. "Just like me. Let's not waste more of our valuable time. The Love case." His beady eyes were trained on Jackson.

"Yes, sir. I'm off the case. I know."

"No, you're not off the case. The investigation is however going in another direction."

"How's that, sir?"

"You will still be the lead detective on this case. You will however get rid of this notion that Mr. Awsum had anything to do with it. It is a waste of time, money, and department resources."

"What do you suggest I do, Major?"

"First of all you have my full support on this thing. It is top priority and I don't want you working on anything else. Your entire caseload has been dispersed. Your lieutenant has seen to that."

Jackson shook his head confusedly. "Not necessary, but okay."

"I'll tell you what is and what is not necessary."

"Yes, sir."

"From here on out you will report directly to Mr. Awsum."

Jackson was stunned. "You've got to be kidding me."

"Do I look like I'm kidding?"

"No disrespect, sir, but you don't think this constitutes a wee bit of a conflict of interests?"

"Mr. Awsum is a professional."

"I have to state my objection to this, Major. It is highly inappropriate and frankly, sir, idiotic." He couldn't believe the gall of the uniformed man before him. "I am removing myself from this case."

"You remove yourself from this case then you remove your gun and badge then remove yourself from this building. Hell, from this state, because you will never work again. You won't even be able to work as a greeter at Walmart when I'm through with you."

"This is bullshit!"

"It's your decision and don't take too long to make it. I'm late for tee off with the Mayor."

"Better things to do, huh?" Jackson loved his job but was dismayed by the position Major Talbert was placing him in. "I still say it's bullshit, but I'll do it."

"I thought you would. Smart man."

Jackson didn't respond. He ground his teeth until they screeched.

The Major wasn't done with him. "One last thing, Jackson. You have a new partner."

***

...damn near impossible

~Cheyenne

Carlene Stone sat in the third row near the front as the pastor concluded his sermon. The organ player tickled the keys of the old organ to cue the choir and congregation for the next song of praise. As the choir began to sing the congregation rose to their feet. It still hurt her to stand on the leg she had been shot in so she remained seated along with an elderly lady sitting a few feet from her. She smiled at the old woman. Carlene felt good. This was the only place she felt truly comfortable and could be herself. No bodyguards, no guns. Just her and God. The more she thought about it, the more she felt a warm sensation stir up inside her. She felt a lump in her throat as she fought back the urge to cry while listening to the choir sing "Open the Eyes to my Heart." Throwing both hands in the air, she let go and gave thanks and praise to her Lord as the tears wet her face.

"Thank you, God!" She cried out as three sharp pains shot through her. Two assaulted her rib cage and the other one attacked her abdomen. Her arms fell to her sides and her head slumped over as the choir and congregation broke into the next song and the church got rambunctious with their stomping and singing. People caught the Holy Ghost and started running up and down the aisles, singing and crying, jumping up and down and passing out. Carlene sat there dead with no one watching. No one noticed except the old lady sitting a few inches from her.

She struggled to her feet clutching her oversized purse. The skinny, gray-haired, old woman wearing sunglasses that covered most of her face and the oversized church hat that the women of the congregation often wore eased her way through the crowd pausing as a young man opened and held the door for her. She walked through the door and down the street passed Carlene's truck and entourage of soldiers picking up speed with each step until she reached her stolen vehicle half a block away. She got into the car, put it into drive, and pulled off. Once she was away from the scene of the crime she removed the hat, wig, and glasses and placed them in a plastic trash bag that was sitting on the passenger seat. A block away from the highway she pulled behind a restaurant and removed her dress. Underneath she was wearing a tank top and cut-off shorts. She took the dress and wiped the Sig P320 with the silencer clean of her fingerprints then dropped both the dress and the gun in a plastic bag as well. Rolling down her window, she tossed the bag into a large dumpster. She looked at her reflection in the mirror and smiled as she turned the radio on to 106.7 WTLC. Niome felt a sense of relief cover her as she put the car in drive and headed for the highway.

***

Danesha ended the call with the press of a button, tossed her phone onto the dashboard, and headed to meet her partner. She felt perplexed yet excited at the same time. She felt like a great ball of energy. Finally, things were falling into place. It wasn't the way that she'd planned nevertheless it was working out. Thoughts of her personal and professional relationship with Aiello ran through her mind. She always felt they were more than just partners. They were family. Hell, he was the only family she had. She'd had a family once. Her girls. Now they never spoke. Now they hunted and plotted on one another. That's the way family goes, she thought as she ran a light through an intersection. She knew they loved one another in a way that only the two of them understood. The more she thought about it, the better she felt about the situation. She was glad he was her partner. It wasn't long before she was pulling into the parking lot of an abandoned warehouse. Aiello's SS was there and he stood leaning against it smoking a cigarette. She nodded at him and he nodded back before sliding the door to the facility open. She drove in and parked. He pulled his car in behind her. She got out and closed the warehouse door.

Aiello got out of his truck and they greeted one another with a handshake. He half-heartedly smiled. He loved her and knew he could never be the one to pull the trigger. He wouldn't have the heart. He knew she knew the rules to this life. Hell, she was the one that had taught him. He was sure that had she known the circumstances she would understand why he did what he had to do. It was all to protect his family.

"Everything been alright with you?" Aiello asked as he placed another cigarette into his mouth, lit it, and took a pull. "You been M-I-A lately."

"Taking care of something. Lining things up. That's all?"

"You found a buyer?"

"Something like that."

Aiello hunched his shoulders. "Something like that? What that mean?"

"I got a situation with this guy. Sort of like a partnership."

"A partnership?" Aiello felt sweat beads forming on his forehead. "I'm your partner. What are you talking about? A partnership with who?"

"Trust me, Aiello. You still have your half of the product?"

"Yeah, I got it." He was becoming agitated. "Why wouldn't I have it?"

Danesha laughed then nudged his shoulder. "Calm down. You need to get you some, man. What you all wound up for?"

"I'm not wound up, Danesha. I just want to know who this guy is. That's all."

Danesha smiled. "He's a silent partner. He wanted to remain silent."

Aiello opened his mouth to speak, but Danesha placed her hand softly on his chest causing him to pause.

"I knew you would want to know who he was so he's coming by to iron some things out," she told him reassuringly. "So relax."

"Iron things out?"

"Business. It's always business."

"Well, can I at least get his name?" Aiello was on edge.

Before she could respond her phone beeped twice signaling that a text message had come through. She looked at her phone, moved to the door, and slid it open. Three black Tahoe trucks pulled into the garage. Men began piling out holding sub-machine guns as Danesha closed the door. Aiello stood alert surprised by the amount of men and artillery present. He counted twelve men total that were beginning to circle the perimeter not leaving room for a tactical advantage if a shootout took place. He and Danesha were completely surrounded. He hoped the meeting went well. He didn't see the chances of coming out of a shoot-out alive with these guys being in their favor. He studied their faces. None looked familiar. They were all Black men, wearing black sweaters, slacks, and dress shoes, topped with black leather jackets and all with freshly shaven heads.

He looked for any sign of which one could be the boss. None stood out so he assumed he was still in one of the trucks. One of the armed men walked back to the last truck to enter as the back window slowly cracked open. All Aiello could see was a glimpse of a Black man wearing a pair of dark sunglasses. It wasn't long before the back door swung open completely and the body was tossed onto the floor bleeding from the neck. Aiello instinctively reached for his sidearm. The empty warehouse echoed with the sound of metal as every gunman in the warehouse simultaneously cocked back their guns at the same time. Aiello paused with his hand still on the butt of his gun. He had yet to unholster it. His eyes met with Danesha's.

"Place it on the floor, Aiello," she advised. "And do it slowly."

He did as she asked. "What is this all about?" He moved towards Danesha, who was now standing near the truck where the body was tossed from.

"You wanted to meet a man. Well, come on over and meet him."

Aiello, now only inches from the body, looked closer at the corpse. He felt his heart drop to his stomach. How? He thought yet remained silent. Aiello watched as the young man with one hand stepped from the back of the truck.

"So this is him huh?" Kendricks asked as he looked Aiello up and down with disgust.

Danesha nodded yes. She stared at Aiello with revulsion in her eyes. Aiello involuntarily flinched fearing that he was about to be shot as he watched Kendricks reach into his inner suit pocket and remove the cell phone. He tossed the phone to Aiello. He caught it, realizing it was his phone that he'd lost at the restaurant after meeting with Nicolai. He realized he'd been crossed. Nicolai had apparently made a deal with Danesha. Aiello laughed. Nicolai got what he deserved, he thought as he glared at the man's slashed, lifeless frame on the ground before him.

"It's me, Danesha." Aiello tried to appeal to the woman. "Aiello... Your partner. You'd do this after all we've been through? Where's the love? Where's the trust?"

"Allowing others to trust you is ideal when dealing in matters of the heart or in business. Relinquishing your trust is dangerous."

"How can you cross me like this?"

"You made it easy. We only cross those who trust us. Betrayal of a stranger is damn near impossible."

Tears rolled down his eyes as he closed them and braced himself for what was coming. He struggled with himself from within to not run, faint, or drop to his knees and beg for his life. He knew this was the end. He listened as he heard the sound of truck doors slam closed and the engine start. He kept his eyes closed as the sound of a truck backing out filled his ears. Immediately after that he heard simultaneous shots ring out as his body jumped and jerked like kernels of popcorn being popped in a pot on the stove. His shredded, bullet-riddled frame laid crumpled next to Nicolai's on the ground.

***

Niome hurriedly had packed her things before Cheyenne made it home. It was time to move on. She was grateful for all that she had done and all that she had taught her but goodbyes were always hard for her. She was surprised that her teacher and newfound mentor was not home. A part of her wished she had been there. She fantasized about the two of them leaving Indiana and maybe starting fresh some place new. It was all a dream thought. She knew Cheyenne didn't like her and that she only tolerated her. She knew there was no way she could ever repay her, but she still felt obligated to do so. After she <u>was all packed and ready to go</u> she unwrapped the yellow diamond earring she'd found in her dead mother's hand which she'd kept tucked in the silk Louis Vuitton scarf. She placed it on the center of the dresser just as her bedroom door opened. She didn't turn but caught off guard she scooped the earring back into her hand. Looking up into the mirror, she stared at Cheyenne's reflection.

"Where you been?" Cheyenne asked still standing in the doorway.

"It's done."

"What's done?"

"The business with Carlene Stone."

Cheyenne stepped into the room. "Done, done?"

"I took care of it."

Cheyenne looked around the room at Niome's bags. "You were leaving without telling me it was done?"

Niome shrugged. "Figured you would find out one way or another."

"You sure it was done?"

"Two kill shots to the lower torso. I watched her slump over. Even if she makes it to the hospital, she won't make it."

"You don't sound like the same kid that was scared to gut a baby rapist a couple of weeks ago."

Niome smirked. "I'm not. You were wrong though."

Cheyenne's brow rose. "About what?"

"I do realize there is no coming back. I did it. I can't change that. Yet the feeling you spoke on... I never felt it."

"Thank God, kid."

"For feeling no remorse? Should I?"

Cheyenne felt uncomfortable. She looked at the floor for a split second then back into the mirror where she found Niome's eyes still trained on her.

Niome spoke firmly. "This is the end for me. I have to leave this place."

"Don't tell me where you're going."

Niome nodded. "What about you? Are you done?"

"Not yet."

"You need me...."

"You don't owe me anything."

"You're Sig."

"Yeah?" Cheyenne braced herself.

"Cleaned it and tossed it."

Niome turned to Cheyenne directly. "I want to pay you."

"You have nothing I want."

Niome stepped to Cheyenne with the earring still clutched in her fist. She extended her arm out to Cheyenne.

Cheyenne took her hand into hers and held it closed. She gave her a hard stare. "I mean it. Keep it. You have nothing I want."

"This other thing you need done... What do you need me to do?"

"Nothing." Cheyenne released her hand and stepped back.

"I want to help."

"Thought you had to leave this place?"

Niome considered it. "Are you putting me out?"

"You can stay or go. It don't matter."

"What do you want me to do?" Niome asked again.

Cheyenne looked at her long and hard before answering. "Get a message to a man."

***

Jackson pulled up to Awsum's mansion only to find Danesha's car parked out front. He hadn't the slightest idea as to what she was doing there, but he knew two things for certain. One, he would find out very soon and two he most definitely wouldn't like it. This entire case had been a headache from day one. Body after body piling up and he was nowhere near finding out who was behind it and why. The one lead he did have got squashed by the powers that be which made him feel even more like a pawn on a chess board. It was only a matter of time before he was sacrificed to save the King. He warily climbed from the car, closed the door, and trekked to the door. Taking a deep breath, he rang the doorbell. It wasn't long before the door was opened and Awsum greeted him.

Awsum stepped to the side allowing Jackson to enter. Jackson walked in closing the door behind him. Following Awsum through the foyer into the living room, he found Danesha standing at the bar sipping a drink. Awsum gestured for Jackson to have a seat. Jackson declined with the shake of his head. He found it strange that two suspects in a murder case were not only involved but also in charge of finding the victim's killer. Jackson wondered just how far up this thing went.

"No need to waste time with the introductions," Awsum stated as he walked around the bar and made himself a drink. "We all know one another in one way or another."

Danesha rolled her eyes.

Jackson frowned at her. "What is she doing here?"

"Major Talbert told you that you would have a new partner." Awsum held up his hands wiggling his fingers in Danesha's face. "Alakazam! Here you are!"

"How'd you like the reporters?" Danesha chimed in with a chuckle.

"You've got to be freaking kidding me? I should've known you were behind that crap."

"Deal with it, Detective," Awsum advised. "Whatever you two have going on put it behind you and work this case. Share your files on the case with her and bring this thing to a close."

"I'm beginning to wonder if it even matters. Why we don't just..."

The doorbell rang and Awsum held up his hand pausing Jackson. "Listen, Detective, I work in a think tank environment where we welcome all ideas and suggestions as long as it is constructive. I advise against wasting everyone's time if it doesn't attempt to move the case forward."

Jackson changed his mind about completing his sentence. Awsum's assistant entered the room followed by Niome. Awsum felt a shortness of breath when his eyes fell upon her. The room fell into an awkward moment of silence.

"I'm in the middle of a meeting," Awsum stated with a fierce tone.

The assistant nodded. "I know, sir. But she has some information for you that could not wait."

"You must be Awsum." Niome stepped toward the man. "Is there some place we can speak?"

Danesha remained silent. She watched Awsum's expression as did Jackson. Jackson's assistant watched them all. Awsum walked towards the door and Niome followed. His assistant stayed in the living room with Jackson and Danesha while Awsum and Niome stepped outside.

"What's this all about?" Awsum asked taking in Niome's appearance.

"I have a message from Cheyenne."

"Go on." He relaxed a little. The girl didn't seem to know who he was so she wasn't confronting him.

"She told me to tell you that it's not done."

"Is that all?"

"No. She also said to tell you its all a part of life." Niome shrugged. "She said that you'd know what that meant."

"Very well, young lady." He stepped closer to her face so that he towered over her. She smelled the alcohol on his breath. "You deliver a message to her for me. It is done when I end it!"

Niome backed away from Awsum.

He grabbed her by the wrist and pulled her back to him. "Don't you come back around here, little girl." He pushed her to the ground.

She scooted back with her eyes still locked on his. Jumping to her feet, she exited the house and rushed to her car. He stood in the doorway and watched as she backed out and gunned it down the street. He continued to look at the car until it was completely out of his eyesight. Awsum took three deep breaths before walking back into the house. Upon reaching the living room, he found his assistant standing guard and Danesha still drinking at the bar.

"Where's Jackson?" he asked.

"He had to use the loo," his assistant replied.

Awsum stepped to Danesha placing his hand around her arm and spoke into her ear. "I'm going to put Jackson on Cheyenne. Either he'll find dirt on her or she'll take him out. Either way this case goes away. You take care of Niome."

"The girl? Why?"

"Just do it or do I need to remind you of our arrangement?"

"Take care of her how, you pathetic waste of human blood and tissue?"

"I don't want to see her again."

Danesha looked up at Awsum with shock.

The look was not missed by Awsum. "Not dead...I just don't want to see her again. Do what you have to."

"I always do. And after this one we're done. I want that hotel footage." She removed her cell phone, pressed a few keys, and sent out a text message.

"See what's taking him so long." Awsum barked at his assistant as he walked around the bar to fix another drink.

The assistant made her way down the hall to the bathroom where Detective Jackson was. Upon reaching the door before, she could knock he stepped out. He looked shocked to see her standing outside of the door.

"They're waiting," she told him. "Let's go."

He didn't reply. He merely followed her back to Danesha and Awsum.

***

Niome had a lot on her mind, why was she even still in the state? Deep down, she knew why. She was alone. Cheyenne was mean most of the time, but she was the only person she knew. She felt that she had grown a lot, but the prospect of going out into the world alone still frightened her. She didn't want to end up like her mother dead some place...alone. She pulled to a stop light and removed the yellow diamond. Looking in the mirror, she put the earring in her ear. A black Mercedes pulled next to her at the light. The guy driving looked to be around her age. He was bald head and was wearing a black leather jacket. He smiled and pulled off when the light turned green. Niome pressed on the gas and passed the guy up. Her thoughts trailed back to her dilemma. She hadn't noticed that the Mercedes was following her as she pulled into a gas station. While she was in the store paying for the gas, he opened the driver's door of the car she was driving and placed a cell phone into the glove compartment. He was out of the car and gone from the gas station before she returned.

***

Danesha was furious as she swerved in and out of traffic. A blunt burned in the ashtray. As sweet as the platinum Kush smelled her appetite for the potent smoke was ruined. Awsum had had his thumb on her for too long. She had the right mind to take him down. Damn the consequences. But she knew that she had too much to lose she reasoned. In due time, she thought. She drove in a hypnotic state as her mind drifted back to where things had all changed for her and her girls.

Years ago when the crew was together she'd gone on a business trip to Chicago with Whip and the others leaving Nicole alone to tend to their business. They had gotten back to town a day earlier than expected. She'd stopped by Nicole's to check on her and to see if everything had gone smoothly with getting the product. When she saw that she wasn't home, she'd immediately gone to Nicole's favorite bar. She knew that more than likely that's where she was. Danesha had seen her car parked and patiently sat outside of the bar waiting for her to come out. She'd watched as Ickie helped Nicole into the car and they pulled off.

Danesha had been steaming that night. She couldn't believe that Nicole was so drunk that she'd fallen prey to Ickie especially when she'd been charged with securing the product. Danesha had followed the two of them to the hotel and was astonished by how Ickie was so focused on getting in Nicole's panties that he hadn't noticed that she was following them to their room. She'd waited a few minutes then unlocked the door with a key she'd swiped from an employee. Nicole was passed out on the bed and Ickie was in the bathroom when she entered. Danesha was attempting to wake her friend up when Ickie came out of the bathroom and spotted her.

It was all kind of a blur for her beyond that point. All she remembered was the two of them yelling and her standing over his dead body sprawled out in the tub. The switchblade she always carried dripped with blood in her hand. The funny thing was through all of that Nicole never woke up. Right then and there Danesha had decided she was a liability. It was Danesha that had removed the drugs and gun from Nicole's bag. She'd dropped the gun on top of Ickie, took the drugs, and left without thinking twice.

Later she'd expected to get a call from one of her girls or Nicole herself from lockup. She even expected a call to help her get rid of the body if nothing else. But nothing had happened for two days. Nicole never mentioned it so neither did she? To Danesha's surprise Nicole had even popped up with the three kilos. Danesha realized she had underestimated Nicole. She was obviously more resourceful than Danesha had given her credit for. But just as things seemed to be leveling out and getting back to normal Awsum popped up with a surveillance tape of her leaving the hotel. He'd admitted that he'd cleaned up the body and that he had something she'd left that would link her to the crime. Danesha was pretty sure she was careful and didn't leave anything, but it was too late. He had already planted the seed of doubt. She questioned herself now, wondering if she actually had left anything behind to implicate herself. She wanted to off him back then, but she couldn't take any chances she wanted the mystery item that she'd left and the surveillance video and any copies made. That was almost twenty years ago. She knew he would ask for something someday. After all that waiting today was the day.

She pulled up to the Condo Cheyenne was hiding out in. She'd already received a text message from Kendricks' guy that she had followed the girl. He had done as he was told and planted the cell phone. She put the car in park and turned the engine off. Removing her phone from her hip, she keyed in the seven digits to the phone. It rang several times then went to voice mail. Danesha reasoned that maybe the girl was already out of the car or had the music blasting and didn't hear the phone. She pressed the talk button. It dialed the number back. The phone rang and rang again, just as she thought it was about to go to voice mail again a voice chimed through the phone.

"Who is this?" The voice was curious and startled.

Danesha assumed it was the girl. "Take the phone to Cheyenne."

"Who the hell is this?" Niome demanded.

"Tell her its Danesha."

"Hold on."

Danesha listened hard. All she heard was muffled sounds. She assumed Niome had the phone to her side walking towards Cheyenne. She heard the two talking but couldn't quite make out what they were saying. It wasn't long before she heard breathing heavy in her ear. She remained silent waiting for her to speak first.

"I'm coming for you," Cheyenne finally said through the phone.

"Are we on bad terms?"

"Are we on bad terms? Seriously?"

"I understand the others."

"But why you, huh?"

"Why me?" Danesha confirmed her question.

"You had a part in it. You all did."

"A part in what?"

"It doesn't matter."

"If you're coming for me I can't stop it. We'll cross that bridge when we get to it. I called you for something else."

Cheyenne laughed. "You seriously called me to ask for a favor?"

"No. I called to do you a favor."

"Sure, why not? What's up? I just told you, you're living on borrowed time and now you want to help me out? Get the hell out of here."

"Believe me or not, I'm going to say my piece and the rest is up to you."

"Speak." Curiosity got the best of Cheyenne.

"The girl."

"What about her?"

"She's playing you."

"Divide and conquer right?"

"Wrong. No head games. She's playing you."

"How's that oh, great savior?"

"She's Nicole's daughter."

"I don't believe you."

"Believe me. Don't believe me. If you are upset about whatever it is that you're angry about and out for blood what do you think is on her mind about the woman that killed her mother?"

"Bullshit."

"Sleep with one eye open. See you when I see you."

"Not if I see you first."

Danesha ended the call.

***

"You get a report back from that DNA sample I asked you to run, doc?" Detective Jackson asked as he placed the box of Dunkin Donuts on the table.

"Where'd you get this sample from?" the medical examiner asked as she removed a manila folder from a desk drawer. Her platform shoes clacked against the cold, concrete floor as she walked across the room to Detective Jackson. She handed him a folder and opened the box of donuts.

"Retrieved it from Awsum's bathroom trashcan." He opened the folder and began reading.

She picked up a donut and bit into it. "Forget I asked. I don't want to know anything illegal."

"Forget about it, doc."

"I was pretty sure the dental floss would have enough saliva on it."

"Well?"

"It did. We got a hit."

"Awsum?" Jackson's eyes lit up.

"Yes. But you knew that he was in the system from when he worked as a guard at the women's prison. Since I knew, it was a part of the

Love investigation I cross-referenced it against fluids found in any open investigations."

"What did you get?"

"A sort of triangle of sorts."

"Excuse me?"

"Look here." She took the folder from Jackson and sat it on the table placing her half eaten donut next to it. Spreading three separate papers on the table side by side she pointed to the first. "This here is the blood from the possible attacker we found in the hand of Nicole Gleman."

"Was he in the system?"

"She."

"A woman?"

"Yes. Cheyenne Cox. Recently paroled from Rockville." She pointed to the paper in the center. "This here is the DNA result from the dental floss and as we already said it is Awsum's." She then pointed to the third piece of paper. "Here we have the blood from the knife that was found in the postal truck identified as the weapon that killed the postman."

"I thought you said no one is in the system for that one."

"They're not. That's what brings us to our triangle. This third unidentifiable person shares genetic DNA markers with the first two."

"They're related?"

"Not just related. These first two are the parents of the third."

"Creating our triangle," Jackson marveled at the findings. "Thank you, doc. I could kiss you right now!"

The medical examiner picked up her donut and bit into it. "I'll settle for the donuts. Thank You."

Jackson scooped up the papers and slid them back into the folder before rushing out of the room, down the hall, and out of the building. Folder in hand he pressed the unlock button to his car and reached for the door handle. He felt a blow to the back of his head and instantly dropped to his knees. He reached for his sidearm as someone stepped on his wrist. Someone else kicked him repeatedly until he blacked out. The last thing he saw before he was kicked in the face and forced into unconsciousness was the face of a bald black guy wearing a black leather jacket.

***

"What was that all about?" Niome asked with her back to Cheyenne looking in the refrigerator.

"What was that about? How in the hell did you end up with this phone? When did you meet Danesha?"

"That's who that was? I don't know a Danesha. All I know is I picked a set of wheels, peeled the steering wheel, drove a few blocks away and checked the glove compartment. You know, just to see if anything I could use was in there. I disabled the tracking system just like you taught me."

"Then what?"

Niome closed the refrigerator and turned to Cheyenne. "Then I went to Awsum's house."

"Who was there?"

"A foreign white girl."

"Who else?"

"Two dudes and a girl. One of the dudes was Awsum."

"So how you end up with the phone?"

"I told him what you said to tell him, he got all pissed and pushed me around and shit."

"Uh-huh."

"I leave, go get some gas, come back and headed here. When I got here, I heard ringing. That's when I answered and brought the phone to you."

"That's all?"

"Yeah."

"You sure?"

"That's everything."

"Still planning on leaving?"

Niome sighed and pushed her hair behind her ears.

Cheyenne felt as if a heavy load had been dropped on her shoulders. She felt hurt and betrayed. Looking at Niome she smiled, stepped closer, and pulled the girl into a tight hug. She whispered in her ear. "I'm sorry about your mother."

Niome felt herself getting choked up, but she didn't want to cry in front of Cheyenne. She fought back the tears. Cheyenne stepped back and looked into Niome's eyes then at the yellow diamond earring shining in her ear. Almost motionlessly, she jabbed a knife into Niome's stomach. Niome clutched at Cheyenne wide-eyed as the woman plunged the knife in deeper.

***

Danesha read the file that Kendricks' men delivered to her. This was exactly what she needed to even the playing field with Awsum. She had to give him credit though. He was a hell of a strategist. He played all of them in one way or another. Cheyenne had to be the worst. Danesha shook her head and laughed thinking about the past.

Cheyenne had introduced him to them. They all told her from the get-go that he was no good but Cheyenne wouldn't listen. Courtney Awsum was a smooth talker from New York. He was always hanging with a British white girl who he claimed to be his sister. He didn't sell the drugs but had the connect and was working as a corrections guard while he went to school for law. Cheyenne started messing around with him claiming him as her own. He screwed over her and it was probably the reason she'd gotten popped off and ended up doing time.

Here it was almost twenty years later and Awsum was still screwing them over. The snake had married Cheyenne's best friend while she was locked up. Danesha actually felt kind of sorry for Nicole and how she got screwed. She knew the truth. Nicole never had a baby. Hell she wasn't even into men. As far as she knew Nicole was still a virgin. Nicole had finally come clean to her about Ickie and the drugs long after the fact. She told her that she owed Awsum.

Awsum, being the dog that he was, was still messing around with Cheyenne after she caught her case and pled out. She was locked up in the same prison that he worked in. This allowed him to screw her over once again. Awsum was always thinking about the future. He'd covered up her pregnancy after the baby was born in the prison by telling her it died during birth then giving the child to Nicole to raise as her own.

Funny how things work themselves out Danesha thought as she sat at the computer in the office to her new home that she'd just purchased in Fishers. Kendricks had given her the money for the dope. In turn, she bought a five-bedroom home. She had yet to sell her old one but at least she was out of sight and no one knew where she lived. She would deal with Li Calzi as soon as the situation with Awsum and Cheyenne was settled.

Awsum kept his word and gave up the video surveillance from the hotel. It was so old and outdated that she was barely identifiable in the film. She ejected the disc from her computer and dropped it in the trash can. She poured a half a bottle of Jack Daniels over it, lit a match, and dropped it in the garbage. All she could do was take his word that he hadn't made any copies. The evidence she supposedly left was just as she thought. A bluff. A ploy to keep her complacent.

She uploaded the files to her computer and emailed them to the Captain. She had spent the better part of an hour convincing her to pull some strings to use the evidence. Danesha told her she didn't want the credit for the bust and that the narcotics department could share it with Jackson. She sent another email then logged off. Her phone rang disrupting her peace.

"Hello?" She was in no mood for discussions.

Cheyenne spoke from the other end. "What you said."

"Yeah?"

"The kid... it panned out."

"Are we cool?'

"We're cool....for now." Cheyenne ends the call.

***

Jackson was barely out of the hospital when he got the call. They had an arrest warrant for Awsum. He couldn't believe it. He didn't know how or why, but it was going down and if he wanted the pleasure of slapping the cuffs on him then, he had to punch it before someone else stole his glory. He had gotten a call from Danesha. She said the bust was all his and he couldn't wait. He couldn't prove it, but he knew Awsum was behind him getting jumped in the parking lot. He would prefer fifteen minutes alone with him but slapping the cuffs on him would have to do. Pulling up to the door followed by an entourage of squad cars, Jackson got out of the car with the warrant in hand and marched to the front door. He rang the bell and Awsum answered the door. Jackson smiled and held up the warrant then immediately handcuffed the man.

***

Lieutenant Monet sat at her desk on the phone with Danesha. A guest sat across from her waiting as she ended her phone call.

"Detective Andrews, I can't prove it now but I know you leaked the information about Awsum and the Love case to the media."

"Why would I do that, Captain?"

"I don't know. Why would you do that, detective?"

"That's the thing, Captain. I wouldn't."

"Remember our little talk about instincts?"

"Yes, ma'am."

"You don't lose them when you move up in rank. You're off the streets until I get to the bottom of this." Captain Monet hung up the phone. "Thank you again for helping with the case."

"I may not be a district attorney for Illinois anymore but I still know some people and all of them owe me favors."

"Again, I'm sorry about your sister."

Black Love tilted his head slightly diverting his glance from the Lieutenant. He stood to his feet.

She rose as well. "How long will you be in town?"

"Until this thing is closed. Would have been here sooner had business in Nigeria."

"Were you and that Lovelace behind rescuing a group of kidnaped school girls from that Islamic extremist group?"

Monet had proved more resourceful than Black had given her credit for. Not many knew about his association with Lovelace. There was no way she could prove it, it still made him wonder how she knew. Black didn't respond. She continued.

"I've heard stories about you, Black."

"Stories?"

"Yes. This isn't Chicago."

"You better believe it."

"You're a longtime associate and confidant but make no mistake about it, Black... if you put us on opposite sides of the law, the gloves will come off."

"Threat noted, Lieutenant."

"No threat. Just being honest. I owe you that much." She extended her hand to shake his.

His phone rang. He paused to remove the phone from his inner jacket pocket and pressed the talk button. "This is Black."

"Mr. Love?"

"Who is this?"

"You don't recognize my voice, brother in law?"

"Awsum?"

"In the flesh, baby."

"How'd you get this number, what do you want?"

"It's not about me. You tell me what I can do for you."

"It's over, Awsum. You're never going to breathe free air again. You're going down for what you did to Ally."

"What I did to Ally? You should be more concerned about Black if you ask me."

"I'm ending this call. Have a beautiful life in prison, jerk off."

"Hold on, Black. Tell Lieutenant Monet I said her time is coming too."

Black walked over to the window in the office and peered out of the blinds. "Where are you?"

"Waiting to post bail. We'll see each other sooner rather than later."

"Looking forward to it."

"It'll be well worth the wait. I won't hold you any longer. By the way that was a beautiful car you had." The call ended.

"What was that about?" Lieutenant Monet asked as she looked out of the window towards the parking lot.

"Our friend Awsum... he...."

A loud explosion erupted from the parking lot. Lieutenant Monet hit the floor clutching at her side arm at the same time. Black stood unmoved as he watched his car burned up in flames.

***

Awsum sat in his cell reading over files from his case. Black had more pull than he had anticipated. He couldn't believe he was denied bail. Half of his accounts were frozen and the other halves were seized. He had money, but it was all cash. Only he knew where it was and he didn't trust anyone else to get it. He was forced to defend himself in court. He was confident he would win, but it was the idea of lost time that bothered him. He set the papers down and stood near his cell bars as he awaited mail to be delivered. It wasn't long before the prison mail courier arrived with a package for him. He looked at the small box oddly wrapped in a ripped brown paper bag. There was no return address. He knew to receive this it had to be from someone with connections. There's no way the prison would allow the package to go to an inmate and not know who and where it came from. He went back into his cell and sat on his bunk. Ripping the paper off he opened the box. The contents didn't look like anything important. It was just a mere handkerchief. He opened it and saw that it was stained with blood. Looking inside the box, he found a small card. His eyes read it twice.

You thought this was over because you're locked up? Wrong. NOW it's over! You took mine from me, I took yours from you. That's your daughter's blood. Thought you might want something to remember her by.

-Cheyenne.

The End

Sneak Peek
Dope Fiction Part 2
Greed between the Lines

A Week Later

Danesha walked into her precinct with all eyes glued to her as she moved towards the Captain's office. She was still on suspension pending an investigation. She could care less. She had another deal with Kendricks going and money was coming in faster than she could count or hide it. She was only there today to drop off her gun and badge. With head held high she didn't give a second look to the female duo of detectives sitting at her and Aiello's old desks. Reaching Monet's office she tapped on the door before walking in.

"Detective," Monet said as she stood to her feet.

Danesha removed her side arm and unclipped her badge from her belt placing them both on her desk. "See you around, Captain." She turned and exited the office.

Holding her head down a slight smirk creased her lips. As she raised her head the familiar sound of thunder erupted in the room. Danesha fell back clutching at her chest with one hand and clutching at her hip where her gun once was with the other. Blood seeped through her fingers and tears filled her eyes. She stared up at Jackson he stood over her with the barrel of his .38 staring her between the eyes. She felt every inch of her skin crawl as shots rang. Three came from behind her from Captain Monet and too many to count flew in front of her from the officers in the room. Jackson's bullet-riddled frame hit the floor with a squishy splat. His eyes were still open and his hand was still clutching the .38. Danesha stared in shock of her own reflection staring back at her in his dead brown eyes.

About the Author

Antwan Floyd Sr. is an avid reader, poet, author, publisher, graphic designer & father. With his own brand of storytelling, he brings a different perspective to the literary world. He launched Bleeding Pen Publishing in 2009 and has since released several titles in paperback and in eBook format. He currently resides in Indianapolis, IN where he is working on his next project.